In a trice Lucille was as naked as the day she had emerged into this amusing world. I had, for the first time, an opportunity to view her beauties, and they were considerable. Her breasts were truly magnificent, boldy jutting cantaloupes with lovely aureoles and firm, stiffened paps. Undoubtedly the just-concluded love ritual with her husband had teased those love-buds into saucy turgidity. Or maybe their upstanding state bespoke her ardour for the continuation of this age-old sport. Her skin was magnificently ivory, except where the sun had lighly bronzed her calves and her beautifully contoured upper arms and shoulders. The whiteness of what remained was, of course, intensified by that contrast. And as her husband stood there looking at her, I could see him beginning to respond once again to the glories of her naked charms . . .

Also available from Headline:

Love Bites

Anonymous

HEADLINE

First published in Great Britain in 1992
by HEADLINE BOOK PUBLISHING PLC

10 9 8 7 6 5 4 3 2 1

ISBN 0 7472 3796 4

Printed and bound in Great Britain by
Collins Manufacturing, Glasgow

HEADLINE BOOK PUBLISHING PLC
Headline House
79 Great Titchfield Street
London W1P 7FN

Love Bites

CHAPTER ONE

I left England, wafted by a favorable wind blowing to the south, and found refuge in a little village in Provence, aptly named Languecuisse—which, for those readers who are not fluent in the French language, is translated to mean "Tongue Thigh." An interesting name although I must say that I did not choose the site purposely; I simply was opportunist enough to let the wind carry me where it would. Autumn was not far off, and the chilly climate of England did not appeal to me since I would have been forced to go into hiding or hibernation, limiting my chances of nourishment and also of diversified contact with interesting people. For even a lowly Flea may have aspirations to culture, mark that well.

The village of Languecuisse was dominated by vineyards where noble wines were pressed from the rich grapes. In all, I should say there were perhaps two hundred people residing in that charming region, for nature had endowed Languecuisse with beauty that delighted the eye of the beholder. Once I landed I found myself in a little valley surrounded almost entirely by rolling hills and protected from the gusty winds that can wreak havoc not only on tender grapes but also on my own kind. The soil was wonderfully fertile, as it must be to produce the lush white and purple grapes whose nearly bursting skins yield the

Burgundies and Sauternes and Chablis which I am told those of means are wont to imbibe. Besides the vineyards, there were carefully tended gardens and hedges, and many plots of vegetables. All this told me at once that the inhabitants of Languecuisse were not starving, and that in turn meant that I should not grow meager and pine away for lack of nourishment. For, if the human race is one of opportunists, then assuredly we Fleas, being part of the divine scheme of things, are equally so; from this you may draw the logical inference that a Flea would rather attach himself to a person goodly in flesh than to one who is lean and jaundiced.

I had arrived, it appeared, just in time for the September harvesting of the grapes, judging from the comments of the beldames whom I heard as I broke away from the friendly breeze that had borne me over the Channel to this exquisite little valley in the heart of France.

I found temporary lodging on the beam of a door to a pleasant little cottage not far from the largest vineyard, and there a plump red-haired woman in cap and apron was gossiping with her neighbor, a black-haired, olive-skinned wench with bold eyes and breasts that strained against the low-cut bodice of her muslin dress.

"Tomorrow, Dame Margot," the plumper one was saying, "we shall see how well the good grapes can be pressed. I myself intend to take part in the contest."

"I trust, then, Dame Lucille, that your wind and stamina will hold out. Your intentions are good, but to stand in a wine vat in the hot sun and tread the grapes even for half an hour would tax a maiden many summers less your own age," was her neighbor's taunting retort.

"Bah," sneered the red-haired matron, "you know not of what you speak. If I am still capable of making my good man Jacques beg for mercy after a few jousts in bed with me. Have no fear that I shall tire when I press the grapes. I have pressed the juice out of his wine-maker on many a night when he was boasting of his prowess, and I could have pleasured even your own handsome husband, to say nothing of half a dozen more."

I have always been amused at the boastfulness of mortals, who always seem to be trying to prove their own superiority. This is, of course, a matter of relative significance, since time has a way of effacing all the achievements of a generation. Now we Fleas are short-lived indeed, and most of us seek to prove nothing except our own right to existence. When you consider that we have more enemies than ever opposed the race of human beings, I modestly say it is little short of a miracle that we survive at all. Not only are the elements arrayed against us, but also birds and alien insects and the animal kingdom from the mongrel dog to the veritable King of Beasts, the lion himself. But we too have ambitions like Man, and that is why we are attracted to his species for our nourishment. For a Flea to sustain himself as I have done on the body of a male or a female requires wit, ingenuity, courage and not a little heroism.

But to return to the scene at hand. This handsome matron of goodly girth and luxuriant auburn tresses who bore the name of Dame Lucille had quickened my interest by declaring to her neighbor that she was extraordinarily competent between the sheets. Her boasts of prowess roused in me nostalgic memories of impassioned embraces in which I had participated both as impartial observer and even as catalyst. I had recently been the cause of an amorous man falling short of his incestuous desires for his niece when, by digging my proboscis into the sensitive covering of his scrotum, I caused him to ejaculate before his weapon could reach the targeted love-chalice of his adorable young niece. I told myself that it might be amusing to stay awhile with Dame Lucille to discover whether her opinion of her own amatory powers was truly deserved. I was also thinking of the descriptions I could collect for the edification and amusement of my readers. I would make good use of my unique ability to slip into supposedly private places unnoticed.

To be sure, since I found myself in a strange new clime and surroundings, the guiding and primal principle of survival was uppermost in my mind. It was essential that I find a source of nourishment, for I was already somewhat faint with hunger as a result of my long wind-borne journey. And the fulsomeness of her fine white flesh seemed to promise a magnificent source.

As I prepared to fly down from my vantage point on the door, Dame Margot, the bold-eyed, black-haired wench, put her hands on her svelte hips and jeered: "Why, as to that, it's easy enough to wag one's tongue where there is nothing to be gained. You know very well that you have as little chance of enticing my Guillaume to your bed as I have of proving to your Jacques that I could exhaust him in half the time you take. So save your energies, good Lucille, for the contest tomorrow."

"Pooh!" the auburn-haired matron put out her tongue in derision. "I was always one to suit action to words. I would willingly exchange husbands with you to prove my boast, but I know that your Guillaume is so afraid of his own shadow and of your nagging that he would not dare come to my bedchamber for a good fucking. Nay, a better fucking than ever he had in his life."

This taunt evidently pricked Dame Margot's wifely pride in a sensitive spot, for her face reddened with anger and she promptly exclaimed, "I will call your bluff and show you up to be a lying shrew! If you succeed in winning tomorrow afternoon, I give you my word that my Guillaume will come to your bedchamber ready to do you service whenever you propose. But I do not think that your Jacques would willingly stand by and watch himself being cuckolded."

"I will take that wager," declared my red-haired hostess (for I had already decided to attach myself to her until such time as I could determine my destiny), "and I will be equally generous. If I win, I will send Jacques to your bed and bid him account to me strictly of your capabilities once his wine-maker is pressed well within your matrix. I warrant you that your Guillaume will be limp and useless in my bed a long hour before my Jacques is used up between your thighs."

"Done!" Dame Margot stamped her foot, her eyes sparkling with angry determination. "But suppose you are not the winner in the grape-treading contest, Lucille? What forfeit will you then pay, you boastful jade?"

While Dame Lucille was pondering her reply, I took advantage of the respite to hop down to her shoulder whence I made my way to her soft white neck, hiding under the luxuriant cascade of auburn tresses which fell nearly to her waist. Her skin was dazzlingly white and her neck was round and delightfully succulent. Having some expert knowledge on the subject, I adjudged her to be approximately thirty years of age, in the full bloom of her wifehood. She evidently felt me, for she put her hand back to her neck and rubbed. But as I had anticipated this maneuver, I had already adroitly crawled over her neck down to her bosom. Between those juicy, round, solid globes I nestled motionless so that she could not feel my presence. The warmth and the sweet aroma of her naked skin delighted me. Although a peasant woman, she was much cleaner than I would have supposed. I have always been a discriminating Flea, and what interests me most is the challenge which I and my brethren must meet in our quest for survival. Now it is easy enough to attach oneself to the body of a man or a woman who has no great liking for hygiene. But when a Flea succeeds in remaining with someone who is not afraid of soap and water, then I say he has truly demonstrated acute perception. I now awaited Lucille's answer, and it was not long in coming: "If I lose, Dame Margot, why then I promise you that you shall fuck with my Jacques whenever it please you and without the least bit of anger on my part—against you or him."

"Why now, that is a fair wager and I will accept it gladly," the black-haired wench smilingly nodded. "And now that we have both spoken so frankly, I do not mind telling you that I have long coveted your husband and wondered how well he could conduct himself atop me. For I think that since I am younger than you, good Dame Lucille, I needs must possess more abundant juices in my slit than you in yours. And, as you well must know, it is not enough to be a trough for a man's spunk, one must also contribute one's own loving flow. A good day to you, but I will not wish you luck on the morrow." And with this, tossing her head, she retired to the cottage next door and banged the door shut.

My red-haired hostess let out a gasp of indignation and remained staring after her neighbor, her hands still on her ample hips, her eyes smoldering with jealous rage. "I will spite that forward hussy if it is the last thing I do! If I win the wager, as I shall, I shall fuck not only her Guillaume to my utter satisfaction, but I shall so contrive that, when my Jacques beds down with that sallow jade, he will have no spunk left for her enjoyment because I shall take it all for myself. Younger than I am, indeed! Why, despite my thirty-one summers, I am still warmer and juicier between the thighs than she with her twenty-seven!"

At this point, I decided to sample her and took a very tiny bite of the white flesh between her big full breasts. It was true, she was most appetizing, and the flesh was as soft as a girl's. The squeal she gave was properly youthful, too. I told myself that for a few days, at any rate, it would be amusing to learn how a Frenchwoman lived and loved. I had always heard that the French were more passionate than the English, so my emigration might well prove to be educational.

When Dame Lucille slapped at herself to alleviate the tiny burning pangs of my quick nibble, I had already escaped to the deep, narrow hiding place of her bellybutton. And when she closed the door of her cottage, she did not know it, but she had given me her hospitality at least for the night.

CHAPTER TWO

Before I proceed to the description of the connubial scenes I was destined to witness on this, my first evening in France, I think it well that my readers understand something of the nature of my species. We Fleas have been much maligned throughout the centuries, principally because we are said to be conveyors of the great outbreaks of bubonic plague. I shall not attempt to contradict the learned men of science and medicine who thus denounce us; I say only that we have conveyed these germs unknowingly, since they are not fatal to us. And I submit that if these same learned men were to examine our annals, they would find that there has never been in all of the Flea history a civil, much less an international, war. I submit that our morality is far less suspect than that of the species which condemns us. But so much for that.

But you may ask how it is that a Flea can survive on the human body without detection and without the constant peril of extermination? Well, let us consider the Flea. In an era when there are complaints of expanding human population and decreasing food supplies for their nourishment, my brothers and I in no way deplete the world's supply of food. Consider that an unfed adult Flea may remain alive a year or more without the slightest nourishment. In some way, indeed, we may be said to resemble the camel in being able to sustain ourselves on a very minimum of nourishment. We adult Fleas have a flat hard-skinned body, very thin from side to side, which permits us to slip between the hairs or the feathers of the animal on which we feed. And our large hind legs permit us to jump as much as thirteen inches horizontally and almost eight inches high. Moreover, we Fleas have instincts that enable us to anticipate the slightest threat to our safety so that we invariably alter our hiding places when danger is imminent. We need not always remain attached to the lovely bodies of young girls and women, whom we have come to admire for their energy and amatory zeal. For example, I myself could have well remained all the night long atop that beam. It was only my innate curiosity—and that is one of the most powerful of all Flea instincts—which made me decide to follow the comely Dame Lucille into her cottage.

Finally, in my own defense, let me add that while there are at least five hundred species of Fleas, almost half of which are found in North America and the West Indies, only a very few are really troublesome or dangerous to man. I am not one of these, happily.

And now that you perhaps understand me better, let me tell you what took place in the bedchamber of the auburn-haired matron whose hospitality I had chosen for my first night in France.

About an hour later, my hostess's spouse came in from his work in the vineyard. He was about forty years of age, lean, bronzed from the sun, with a strong jaw, a long nose, and a high forehead. His brown hair was liberally streaked with gray and his expression was dour. Yet you would have thought him the most handsome Casanova in all the world from the way his good wife welcomed him. With much cooing and giggling, like that of a schoolgirl, Dame Lucille hastened to him, flung her arms exuberantly around his neck and bussed him resoundingly on the mouth and cheeks and eyes and nose. "Mon amour, how did it go today?" she inquired as she continued to hold onto him and to arch her loins against his in a most suggestive manner.

"Well enough, ma belle," he remarked in a gruff voice while his hands roamed over her back and down to her plump, spaciously rounded buttocks, which he began to squeeze with lingering enjoyment. "It will be quite an event tomorrow afternoon. Master Villiers has promised that the winner of a contest, she who treads out the most wine from her vat, shall have a month's rent free as well as a dozen bottles of the finest wine."

"Never fear, dear Jacques," his wife purred as she wriggled about in his embrace, "I shall win the prize for you, my dear husband."

"Now *that* I do not expect of you, Lucille," he chuckled, as he at last disengaged himself from her embrace. "Go get my supper, that's a sweetling. With all due respect, I do not much suppose you can best the maidens who will compete against you. They are much younger and stronger in the limb, for all your good intentions. But I am well satisfied with you, nonetheless."

With this, he gave her a lusty clap on the behind which made her squeal, and in great good spirits he strode off to his own chamber to remove his working clothes, which were soiled and stained from his work with the grapes.

When he returned, I saw somewhat to my surprise that he was clad only in his nightshirt. At first blush this seemed strange since the sun was only just setting and it certainly was not time to retire for the night. But I quickly divined that the worthy vintner was suffering from the pangs of two different hungers and wished merely to be in a state of readiness for the satisfaction of both. His auburn-haired spouse hovered about him like a cooing dove as he seated himself at the table, nor did she think it amiss that his attire for the evening repast was so informal. She brought him first a bowl of lentil soup, together with a crusty loaf of freshly baked bread and a bottle of red wine. Graciously he deigned to pour out two glasses, one of which he took and clinked to hers.

"May you have luck tomorrow, ma mie," he chuckled as he circled his right arm around her graceful waist and hugged her to him. After he had taken a sip of the wine, he put his lips to the bodice of her thin dress and nuzzled the luscious curve of one of those magnificent breasts of hers. "Yet on the other hand," he added, giving her a jocular wink, "mayhap I should not wish you such, for you know it is the custom of the patron who owns the vineyard in which we all toil to fuck each harvest time with her who is declared the most puissant squeezer of grapes. Hence, Lucille, if you should win on the morrow, I should be compelled to accept cuckoldry from him who pays me my wages. Do you still tell me that you wish to come off victorious in a matter that concerns my own husbandly honor?"

At this, the buxom Lucille promptly left her place on the other side of the table, went around to him, clasped her fair white arms about his chest and lovingly rubbed her cheek against his as she purred, "Dear Jacques, do you think me a faithless trollop, then? I warrant you, even should I win as I mean to—if only to spite that harpy Margot next door—Monsieur Villiers shall not pluck my flower nor rob me of my wifely virtue. Do you not know that a woman has ways of denying a man that which he seeks to take possion of between her thighs? There are manners and methods of exciting the good patron so that he will lose all his juices before he manages to pour them out into that funnel which nature gave all women to have as the receptacle of man's passion."

This salacious retort pleased Jacques mightily, for he roared with laughter and clapped his good wife resoundingly upon her ample buttocks. Breaking the crusty loaf, he tore off a chunk and took an enormous bite, washing it down with the red wine. His eyes sparkled as he watched his handsome spouse return to her seat.

Although they both spoke French—with that softly slurred dialect which is famous in Provence—I understood them well. The erudition of a Flea is assimilated much as his nourishment; herein is one advantage that my species possesses which man cannot attain save by assiduous study. It suffices for a Flea to bite the flesh of a human to acquire, at that moment, a comprehension of the language which that provider of nourishment ordinarily speaks. In fact I had acquired some sense of the language while still back in England some little time before I met the fair Bella and Julia. It happened that I had partaken of the flesh of a handsome Parisian actress who, during her sojourn in London, had become the mistress of an Earl to whose person I was then temporarily attached. I mentioned all this not out of boastfulness—for such is not the nature of a Flea, that being an attribute reserved for mankind—but so that my readers will not doubt the veracity of my tale. I think also that my readers may envy my kind, for surely it is far easier and more delightful to acquire the knowledge of a language by sinking one's proboscis into the white flesh of a fair damsel's thigh or breast or haunch than to ponder over a guttering candle and learn another tongue word by laborious word.

But I digress. There is little need to relate what went on during the rest of the evening meal, though there was much bawdy conversation and laughter as Jacques and Lucille Tremoulier discussed the forthcoming wine-pressing contest and the candidates against whom she would be opposed the next afternoon. I listened with great interest and amusement. It is said that women are catty by nature and that they rip to pieces even their best friends once within the intimacy of their own chambers. Yet I tell you that men are equally verbose when it comes to denigrating their neighbors. The worthy Jacques went into rapturous and somewhat lascivious expatiations on the charms of the women of the village, and it was evident from this that he had already looked with lustful eye upon Dame Margot, that bold, black-haired wench who had made the wager with Lucille.

However, I could not deduce from all his remarks whether he'd had actual carnal knowledge of the beauties of whom he spoke so knowingly. Lucille even added her own evaluations, and I was reasonably certain that she was not perversely acquainted with these damsels and matrons. She and Margot, it appeared, had once bathed together naked in a little stream down by the mill, and she informed her worthy husband that Margot's thighs were leaner than hers, and that there was a dainty brown, oval-shaped birthmark just to the left of the wench's bellybutton.

At the end of the repast, Lucille served her husband a glass of brandy with his coffee and took one for herself also. The good stew, the crusty bread, the red wine, had put them both into a convivial state, and their language was entirely uninhibited as a result. "Tell me, chéri," Lucille purred as she took a sip of her brandy, "if you had your choice of all the women in this village with my leave, with whom would you desire most to make love?" (Here I might observe that she used the vulgarism, "plonger ton vit," which, roughly translated, means "plunge your cock into.")

"Now of course, ma belle," Jacques remonstrated with a cajoling smile, "it is understood that you will bear me no ill will if I speak my mind. For you know that I am as faithful as any husband to his wife here in Languecuisse."

He was, in truth, a masterful diplomat because his remark implied that he was no better or worse than any other man in this little village, and I am certain that continence and chastity could not be uppermost in a land where the sun is warm and the wine is red and stirring to the senses and there is so much white flesh abundantly revealed. But Dame Lucille did not attempt to read any second meaning into his seemingly innocent statement, for she laughingly avowed, "I have told you that you may speak without fear of my wifely anger, dear Jacques. Pretend, therefore, that you are the ruler of a mighty suzerainty and that to your beck and call come the fairest maidens from every corner of the globe. Whom then would you select to baiser?" (This word, which means "to kiss," also means "to fuck." This is why we say that the French language is full of double entendres.)

He nursed his chin for a moment and frowned, lost in thought. Then he chuckled and declared, "Why, then, since I am the lord and master of all I survey, I should summon the fair Laurette Boischamp. Of a certainty, she is the loveliest in all this village, and her flower has not yet been plucked, if I am not mistaken. Yea, I would fuck her, and fuck her right well."

"For your sake, Jacques, I hope you speak aright," Lucille banteringly responded, "for though I have given you leave to express your mind, if I should ever discover that it was you who robbed that charming hoyden of her virtue, I should drub you soundly and deny you access to my bed for a good month. Harken well my warning on that score. But since we are speaking of imaginary things, do tell me why your choice rests upon Laurette."

"Pour me yet another glass of strong brandy, ma

belle, and I will tell you why," he chuckled. And when Lucille had complied with his wish, he took a long sip of that potent cognac and exclaimed, "Ah! If ever I fail to answer the summons to your bed, dear Lucille, you have but to give me this cognac to rouse my torpid blood to action!

"Now, as for Laurette Boischamp, this is why she would be the first lady of my harem, were I a pasha. She is but nineteen, she is innocent, her hair is golden and thick and soft and silky, and it falls over two of the sweetest, plumpest breasts in Christendom. You could span her waist with both your hands, and yet her hips are round and firm and sturdy, ample enough, I am certain, to support the thrusts of the boldest prick in all the world. These warm summer days, as she does not always wear hose, I have seen her down by the brook washing the laundry, and I will confess to you, Lucille, that her skin is as white and pure as fresh milk. Her ankles are delicate and gracefully shaped, and her calves are fine and slender but with a hint of ardent curves above."

"I trust you have seen no more than that," Lucille sharply interrupted, glowering at him with her cat-green eyes, "or else, even though I have given you leave to speak your mind, your prick will have no work tonight! Is her skin milkier than mine, then?"

He coughed, then sought refuge in his glass of brandy to distract himself so that he could take time to weigh his answer.

At last, wheedlingly, he placated her thus: "Why, as to that, ma mie, I speak only of conjecture. For I saw only the beginnings of her calves as she squatted down there by the brook to take the sheets from her chaste bed and to beat them with a rock. As she leaned forward, I could see only the faintest glimpse of that enticing valley between her two snowy globes, but I tell you that yours are full, luscious and ripe, solid to the grip of my fingers, and I would prefer them to those of any untried maiden's. But it is man's nature always to covet that which he does not possess, and though I am faithful to you and lust for you heartily, as you well know, my beautiful Lucille, I will admit that there are moments when I am fucking you that I close my eyes and imagine that it is the tender Laurette who groans beneath my weight."

"Well, I will not be too irate with you, my worthy husband, for that is a truthful remark and you would not be much of a man if you were not tempted by that charming hoyden. Besides, she is beyond your grasp, for her parents wish to wed her to your employer, the good Monsieur Claude Villiers."

"I know that well, and it is a great pity. Monsieur Villiers is nigh unto sixty if he is a day, and his way of wooing a maiden is to skulk about and try to pinch her bottom. I warrant you, when he finally brings her to the marriage bed, his prick will be shriveled up and worthless."

"I have no doubt of that either, but look to you that you do not seek to furnish her that upstanding prick which she is denied," Lucille tartly declared. "Moreover, though you may not know it, she already has a young swain by the name Pierre Larrieu, who is her own age. He is an apprentice to the same Monsieur Villiers, and they say that he is a bastard. He would not be able to wed her in this village, you may be sure. But if Laurette were wise enough to taste the pleasures of the flesh before she is bedded to that sour, withered old bottom-pincher, I would say that she would prefer young Pierre to you, competent though you are when fucking between a woman's thighs."

Jacques Tremoulier rose from the table and smacked his thigh with a guffaw. "Woman," he bellowed, "with all this talk of pricks and thighs and white skin, you have bewitched me! It is time we were abed! Strip down to your nightshift, then, and join me in the jousts of love, where I will prove that I am as devoted to you as even I was on our wedding night!"

CHAPTER THREE

All this while, I had reposed in the warm little grotto of Lucille's bellybutton, basked in that soft, intimate niche and enjoying my repose while my senses were titillated by the ribald discussion between this worthy married couple. I must confess that I was intrigued by the prospect of discovering how the French method of copulation differed from the English version.

The connubial bedchamber was spacious and most of the room was taken up by an enormous bed with four posters and a canopy. I confess it was more elegant than I would have expected in the abode of a humble worker in the vineyard, but Dame Lucille managed to satisfy my curiosity almost the moment she entered, her arm around her husband's waist and her cheek pressed tightly to his: "I never cease to give thanks to my dear Aunt Therese for this magnificent wedding present. Your employer, old Monsieur Villiers, is surely the richest man in all the province, I have no doubt of it, but I do not think that even he possesses so find a bed for fucking. His poor young bride will, I fear, not lie half so comfortably as we when her wifely time is come."

"You speak wisdom as always, dear Lucille," he chuckled as he turned to face her and squeezed her buttocks with avid lubricity while his lips traversed her cheeks and nose and eyelids. Already I could discern a

noticeable bulge against his nightshirt at the very
juncture of his thighs, and I declare that its formidable
size struck me with admiration and at the same time
no little compassion for its red-haired recipient, who
would be obliged to accept its girth and length within
her delicious cunt. "But it is not the bed that will
matter to her, but the size of her husband's deplorably
useless prick. Now, were she fortunate enough to be
bedded with a man of parts like myself, Lucille, she
would know nothing but bliss, as you shall at once!"

With this, stooping, he grasped the hem of her
nightshift and lofted the thin garment to her waist and
pinned it with one grasping hand, while with the other
he raised his nightshirt. I could then look upon the
magnitude of his weapon. The head of it was
remarkably elongated, like a plum that has been
squeezed a moment too long in the process of being
plucked from its stem. The shaft itself bulged; dark,
angry blue veins writhed under the tightly drawn, thin
skin. His balls were heavy, gnarled and prodigiously
hairy, and indeed this massive weapon sprang from a
hiding place of thick, already graying fleece. But there
was nothing aged about the weapon itself, as Lucille
instantly observed by means of her sparkling eyes and
stifled gasp of "Ohh! It is true that you still desire me,
my husband. And in my gratitude, I will take all you
have and leave you nothing for such hoydens as young
Laurette or that wagging-tongued shrew, Margot.
Observe how eagerly my little slit awaits your
bludgeon!"

With this, she took both forefingers and applied
them to the fleshy, plump lips of her orifice. It, too,
was thickly downed with dark, reddish curls which
nearly hid the aperture. But once the lips came into
view, I could see that they were exquisitely pink and
soft and entreating, and also I perceived a suspicious
moistness which presupposed that the worthy woman

was already anticipating her connubial blessing.
Moreover, the way she wriggled her bottom slowly
back and forth said eloquently that she longed to be
fucked by that huge prick, to feel it filling her to the
utmost as he drove it in her up to the hilt.

"Hurry, then, for I ache to feel myself within the
clutch of your sweet cunt," he panted.

Lucille needed no further encouragement. She
kept one forefinger to pry open her eager slit whilst
she used the other hand to fondle the enormous
weapon which he presented to her. Her fingers were
small and dainty and I can imagine how soft their
touch must have felt upon Jacques' admirably
distended weapon, for he at once groaned, "For our
first bout of the evening, ma belle, do not hold me off
or tease me too long. You know well that one has
more staying power on the second course."

"Oui, c'est bien vrai," Lucille purred with a smile
on her full rosy lips. Retaining hold of his ramrod, she
guided it against the moist, pink cleft which her
forefinger had readied for his entry. He uttered
another groan and grasped hold of her voluptuous
bottom as he drove himself forward to the hilt in a
single mighty stroke. Lucille uttered a sob of delight
and flung her arms around him. There they stood,
their nightclothes rolled up about their waists, glued
together by what the learned Greek philosopher Plato
once described as "the polarity between the sexes."

From my perch nestling inside her bellybutton, I
could observe everything. The pink, plump lips of her
orifice seemed to be drawn back as he burrowed
himself to his very balls within her womb. Their bellies
touched as did their thighs, and a shivering paroxysm
seized them both as their mouths fused in hot
communion. Then slowly he drew himself out almost
to the very tip and there was a sucking sound as the
moist recesses of her matrix grudgingly released his

weapon, straining every wily inner muscle with which the female is so lovingly endowed in the aspiration of bringing him back swiftly to her bower.

For all his furious eagerness, I had to commend him for his powers of self-control. He prolonged the moment of return until Lucille began to wriggle like a fish on a hook, for in truth such she was, so ably harpooned by his vigorous lance. While his fingers dug into the plump cheeks of her bottom, she squirmed and groaned and arched and writhed in the most persuasively lascivious way until, in his own time, Jacques surged himself forward and buried himself to his hairs. Her gasp at this action was raucous with pleasure, and her glazed eyes rolled up into her head. Her fingernails drove into his back, tearing through the stuff of his nightshirt, and her tongue voraciously entered the play between his lips and rubbed and probed with furious abandon.

Once again he drew back to the very tip of his sword, but this time Lucille was too impatient to let him dally with her enjoyment. With an impatient, exacerbated gasp, she ground herself against him in an agony of desire and thus impaled herself upon his blade until she had taken all of it within her hot, moist channel. He set his teeth against the maddening caress of her mobile sheath, for I am certain that her vaginal scabbard was convulsively clenching along his weapon as if she meant never to let it go. He proved this a moment later by suddenly quickening his pace and ramming her with four or five devastating lunges, each of which drew a cry of rapture from his partner in the play of love.

And then, with a final cry of ecstasy, he drew himself back a last time then thrust home and bubbled out all his essence deep within Lucille's welcoming canal of love. Her body jerked and twisted as her own flow answered his, merging as do two rivers in their abundant reunion. Their first foray was at an end.

Good Dame Lucille emitted a long sigh of contentment. When it was over, she bussed her husband on the mouth, saying, "That was a good beginning, my adored husband. But it will take much more to satisfy my passions, so undress us both so that we can be skin to skin and take our joy of each other through the night."

He countered banteringly, "Right willingly will I accept your offer, my dear wife, but are you not afraid that all this will exhaust you for the morrow? I should not wish to stand by and see some chit of a girl, like perhaps that Laurette, win the contest and have the spectators jeer at your failure."

"I will still be trampling grapes when Laurette's thighs give way as she yearns for the soft repose of her virginal bed," the auburn-haired matron laughed. She then unbuttoned his nightshirt and drew it off his lanky body and I perceived that he had a good deal of matted hair over his chest, an ideal resting place for me should I require it during the ensuing fray. For, judging from the gleam which shone from their eyes, I had no doubt that they meant to enjoy their marital life to the fullest extent this night. It would be a heated duel, a warm welcome indeed after the chilly fog of London!

The worthy Jacques returned the compliment and in a trice Lucille was as naked as the day she had emerged into this amusing world. I had, for the first time, an opportunity to view her beauties, and they were considerable. Her breasts were really magnificent, boldly jutting cantaloupes with lovely aureoles and firm, stiffened paps. Undoubtedly their just-concluded ritual had teased those love-buds into a saucy turgidity. Or maybe their upstanding state bespoke her ardor for the continuation of this age-old sport. Her skin was magnificently ivory, except where the sun had lightly bronzed her calves and her beautifully contoured upper arms and shoulders. The whiteness of what remained was, of course, intensified by that contrast. And as her husband stood there looking at her naked charms, I could see his limp penis begin at once to rise in salutation to such glorious enticement.

I had already learned one thing during my journey from one continent to another: while the English might depend on tactile stimulation to be roused to erotic readiness, it sufficed this French peasant to behold his naked wife, which sight at once restored him to full plenitude of animal spirits. He dipped a cloth into a ewer on a table beside the bed and sponged both his cock and his wife's bushy orifice, a procedure which excited them both considerably, as could be seen from the wriggling undulations of Dame Lucille's spacious hips and his own muscular limbs. Then, as gallantly as any courtier, his arm about her satiny waist, he escorted his mature and beautiful spouse to the connubial bed and made her lie down upon it. He bade her raise her knees and spread them well apart. He then stood feasting his eyes on the delicious spectacle of the thick, dark-reddish curls through which peeped the love-swollen pink petals of her cunt. Then he knelt down on the bed, bowed his head between those robust, wonderfully curved snowy thighs, and applied a sucking, noisy kiss to her slit.

Dame Lucille uttered a groan of bliss and clenched her thighs convulsively together to clamp him there as a sweet prisoner of love to her secret bower. He was nothing loath to have this done and his hands roamed over the upturned cheeks of her voluptuous bottom, pinching and patting and stroking those ivory globes till at last he boldly applied a forefinger down the shadowy groove which parted those Calliphygian beauties and arrived at the crevice, which was the rear entry to paradise and which I have observed that many a man seems to prefer to that which Venus blesses for the rites of love. Jacques deftly inserted his finger to the knuckle, all the while covering her mount with impassioned kisses.

I could see at once that the Gallic manner of copulation had inventiveness to commend it. Even this humble wine-maker was aware of the basic tenet of fornicatory pleasure: To give is more blessed than to receive, and in turn greater blessings are bestowed upon the giver thereby.

For, indeed, if connection between the sexes was limited to the thrusting of a penis within the boundaries of a vagina, a narrative such as mine would be dreadfully redundant. But it was precisely by such nuances as Jacques now proceeded to the second tourney that made me give thanks that I had indeed caught that fair wind to Provence.

I deemed it best at this point to transfer my hiding place to Dame Lucille's tresses, whence I could espy the entire procedure with a panoramic view. At once I could perceive from the twitchings of the auburn-haired matron's belly that she was responding to the sweet kisses which her husband pressed upon her furry groove. Her knees were still arched up and her fair white thighs clamped tenaciously about his cheeks to hold him sweet captive to her bidding. Yet the muscles of those round, full thighs shivered and spasmed in the most voluptuous manner, as did her buttocks—for of course he still plied his forefinger to and fro within the dainty rosette of her nether channel. Thus dually stimulated, she was in a veritable seventh heaven of rapture, as was told also by her cooing little cries and whimpering gasps which made enchanting music in this humble bedchamber.

At last she could bear this Tantalus no longer. Swinging wide her knees, she entreated him dulcetly to enter her forthwith. Her husband did not need a second invitation. As he knelt up, I saw that his cock was formidably taut and bulging with renewed zeal to put her to the test. He looked down on the heaving turrets of her bosom, and his other hand cupped one of those luscious globes and kneaded lingeringly while he continued the gentle in and out movement of his delving forefinger. Next, this worthy wine-maker crawled forward on his knees, and crouching adroitly, engaged just the tip of his swollen tool against the moist and palpitating lips of Dame Lucille's ardent slit. Thereupon he began to rub in circular fashion all around the mount of Venus, tantalizing his passionate wife almost to the point of frenzy. Her head began to roll back and forth on the pillow, her eyes were enormously dilated and glazed, and her nostrils flared and shrank like those of a mare in heat awaiting the stallion.

I could not but applaud his preparations for so harmonious a copulatory encounter. And his entire preparation recalled to me that excellent maxim which should be part of the credo of every aspiring lover: When the beloved is passionately lusted for, the male should at once relieve his pent-up longings by a swift act, since, once this is done, nature endows him with greater staying powers for the second and enchantingly prolonged bout. There are those men of little faith who, having ejaculated prematurely because they are undone by the beauties of their feminine partner, deplore their own failing and give up the battle, but they are fools! Let the true lover take heart from what I relate of what took place between Dame Lucille and her worthy lord and master, Jacques, in this obscure village of Provence. Let him remember that, just as faint heart ne'er won fair lady, just so meek cock ne'er was granted true opportunity to show its prowess.

But these two did not need my somewhat

sententious Flea's philosophy; it seemed already to have been inborn within their natures. Dame Lucille at last extended a soft white hand to take amorous hold of her husband's swollen shaft, which to my impartial gaze appeared to be fully as huge as at their first coition. For a moment or two, she tantalized herself by guiding its angrily reddened tip all over the soft crannies of her mount, so that every inch of those greedy, pink, plump love-lips might have their fulsome share. Then, with an eager gasp, as she squirmed her buttocks forward, she guided him between the palpitating petals of her grotto, half raising her head from the pillow and staring at him with loving gaze as she entreated, "Oh, baise-moi le plus fort que tu peux!"

I am certain that no spouse in all of Christendom ever heard more inflammatory appeal, for the luscious matron was, to translate for my readers once again, begging him to "fuck me as hard as you can." He sank down slowly, cushioned upon her fair white belly, his chest mashing down the proud rondures of her panting bosom and her arms clasped him 'round the waist and locked him to her, while her naked legs instantly clamped over his backside so that she might be well mounted for the ride to paradise which lay ahead.

Grasping her nape with his left hand, Jacques foraged under her buttocks with his other hand so that he might restore his forefinger to that tighter, more mysterious channel which he had already exacerbated in the prelude to their amour. Dame Lucille welcomed this restoration with a moan of delirious joy and fused her mouth to his. Then he began a slow and deliberate penetration of her tender parts, so leisurely, indeed, that one might think he was astride a slow mare ambling off on a long winding road which had no end. She matched his gait with a delicious cohesion, not hastening any more than he, but it was evident from the flexing of her muscles that she savored each long slow dig within her groove of pleasure. His finger probing between her buttocks matched this rhythm also, thus rousing the auburn-haired matron to even greater bliss than she had tasted on their initial sally into the realm of Cythera. She began to babble incoherent words, her eyes shining with lust and her fingers clawing at his lean, sinewy back. Her plump ivory thighs incessantly shifted over his backside so that every nook and cranny of her inner labyrinth might feel the goading, rasping gouge of his weapon.

I knew that both of them were in superb fettle for their dalliance, and I was certain also that Dame Lucille would acquit herself as honorably in the wine vat trampling out the grapes before the spectators as she now squeezed her husband's potent wine-maker between her ivory thighs. So wishing to broaden my comprehension of the amorous proclivities of her rival, Dame Margot, I reluctantly took my leave of this worthy couple and flew out through a crack in the windowpane to visit the cottage next door, where Margot and her vaunted Guillaume were doubtless allaying their own carnal beatitudes.

CHAPTER FOUR

No sooner had I entered the cottage belonging to black-haired, olive-skinned Dame Margot and her as-yet-unseen marital partner, Guillaume, than I found the two of them already lustily engaged in almost the same manner in which I had left Lucille and Jacques. There were, however, notable disparities in their manner of procedure as opposed to their good neighbors. To begin with, their bed was by no means so huge and ample, but much narrower and lower. It rose to about the height of mid-thigh. This, of course had its tactical advantages, since if the two of them were swooning in each other's arms, they had only to shrink down easily and they would find themselves sweetly couched, ready for coitional repose.

Margot was indeed a comely wench, now that I could see her stark naked. She appeared to be perhaps an inch or two taller than Lucille, but this height might well have owed to the supple length of her gracefully contoured thighs and sinuously high set calves. It was a moot point, though, since I did not have them both there to compare at the same moment. Her breasts were closely spaced and beautifully conical, like two ripe, firm pears jutting out their dark coral tips to amorous lips and tongue, and her waist was as slim as that of a young girl's. I found a pleasurable contrast in the smooth, warm olive tinting of her skin as opposed to the ivory sheen of Lucille's. She lay on her left side, turned toward her mate, her left arm loosely embracing his shoulders while her right hand caressed what, at first sight, struck me as an even more able weapon than that which Jacques possessed. Her slit was not at all visible to me from my vantage point at the top of the headboard of the bed. It was entirely shrouded by a forest of thick, black curls which ran even along the perineum and toward the amber groove which cleaved her impudently jouncy oval-shaped buttocks, as well as reaching nearly to her navel, which was wide and shallow and in itself a tempting niche for amorous dalliance.

Guillaume was a jovial rogue, with a small, pointed, dark brown beard and moustache whose ends widely curled upwards and were stiff with wax. His brown hair was curly like a boy's and his twinkling blue eyes and full, fleshy lips gave evidence of a sanguine temperament. He was a robust man of about thirty summers, so far as I could determine, with powerful thighs and calves, strong shoulders and a vigorous chest. But most vigorous of all was the object of his consort's attention.

It seemed somewhat shorter than the prick of Jacques Tremoulier, but I vow that it was thicker by a goodly quarter of an inch at least. Guillaume Noirceau had not been circumcised, so the foreskin formed a natural protective cowl over the meatus. Yet now, thanks to the stroking which Dame Margot imparted, the fold of skin was stretched tightly and bared the tip. The lips through which his spunk would flow were puckering with avid desire, and they were exaggeratedly large. Judging also from the size of his thick and hairy balls, I felt that Dame Margot had no cause to bemoan the priapic capabilities of the spouse which Heaven had bestowed upon her.

"I swear, dear Margot, that if my prick were not so eager to plunge back into that tight, hot cunt of yours a second time, I should be quite content to let you draw forth my seed by the magic of your soft slim fingers," he told her in a hoarse voice.

"But we have all the night ahead of us, my beloved husband, and you are certainly virile enough to enjoy many such returns to my loving cunt and still be able to spare one goodly spurt for my little hand," she bantered. "Moreover, I have so boasted to my dear neighbor and friend, Lucille, that I feel you owe me a happy verification of my claims on your behalf."

"Oh, so you and Dame Lucille have been discussing the secrets of our bed, have you now? Take care, Margot, a wagging tongue sometimes earns a good thrashing. Tell me why I should not now deny you the pleasures that your itching, burning cunt so covets, but instead use a good stout stick across your impertinent backside!"

"Do not be vexed with me, dear Guillaume," Margot wheedled as she tightened her left arm around his shoulders, while her other hand busied herself with fondling his now ferociously turgid cock. "You know that she and I have entered the grape-trampling contest on the morrow, and she is so certain of victory that she made a wager to which I had no recourse but to counter."

"Tell me of this wager then."

"Right willingly, dear Guillaume, but first give me a loving kiss and rub the tip of your prick hard against my burning little cunt, so that I may delight in advance of the joy you mean to have with me," Margot coaxed. Her good husband graciously complied with this request and his hand squeezed her resilient buttocks as she squirmed passionately against him, their lips meeting in a long and soulful kiss.

I had already perceived the delicious little crown birthmark shaped like a tiny egg to the left of Margot's belly, exactly as Lucille had told her husband, Jacques.

But I found also that Dame Lucille, in the manner customary to women who gossip, was somewhat malicious in describing Margot's thighs as being a "bit lean." I found them quite the contrary, being long, supple, beautifully and responsively muscled, the superb portals through which a man might enter the paradise he sought.

"Why, now, Guillaume, my beloved," Margot cajoled after the kiss and the requested rubbing of his cock-tip against her cunny had been accomplished, "she was so boastful of winning that she said she would send her husband to my bed so that I might press his prick soundly within my cunt, and so I, in turn, gave her my word that you would go to her bedchamber ready to do her service whenever she proposed if she emerged victorious tomorrow afternoon."

"Now I am not so certain how this involves my husbandly honor," Guillaume frowned.

But the black-haired wench was as cunning as she was amorous, for she taunted him with Lucille's remarks: "Do not be vexed, my dear husband. Do you know what that hussy had the temerity to boast? Why, that you would be limp and useless in her bed a long hour before her husband was used up between my thighs!"

"She said that?" Guillaume bellowed in a voice of rage, and his eyes flashed indignation at the affront. "Well, then, I will abide by the terms of the wager, but you see to it that you win tomorrow, Margot, or you will have a drubbing you will not soon forget. Besides, there is the matter of a dozen bottles of the finest wine, and also the month's rental on our cottage if you emerge the winner."

"I know that well, dear husband, and I am so confident of victory that I will give two of those bottles to Dame Lucille so that she may drink your health and tell all within hearing that you are the best fucker in the whole village of Languecuisse!"

"And you will not be vexed with me if I bed that red-haired slattern?" Guillaume anxiously inquired.

"Nay, my dear husband, no more than you will be angry with me if I prove that Jacques Tremoulier has little staying- and much less standing-power in comparison with your magnificent prick."

Oh, the casuistry of women, especially of this black-haired, olive-skinned wench from fair Provence! Thus had she gained permission for herself to seek out adulterous joys (which I have no doubt she had long secretly yearned to taste!) whilst at the same time offering her bemused consort a chance to discomfit her neighbor and friend, Dame Lucille. One might apply the English proverb of eating one's cake and having it too, for such was Dame Margot's wily purpose in conceiving such a wager and in phrasing it just so to Guillaume.

At any rate, the prospect enchanted him, for he plunged himself to the very hilt inside her cunt and then delved a finger into the furtive rosette between the cheeks of her flossy, resilient bottom, thus granting her ecstatic joy.

Their mouths met in a fierce merging, and I could hear the slushing of their tongues as the one plied the other with feverish ardor. Dame Margot locked her supple arms around her mate's brawny shoulders and gave herself up joyously to the joust. As for Guillaume Noirceau, he must have counted himself the most fortunate of husbands to have so loving and complaisant a wife, who would of her own free will permit his straying from her bed to that of her beauteous neighbor, Dame Lucille. Perhaps it was the thought of fucking the latter which added vigour to his thrust, as well as the tight enclaspment of Dame Margot's vaginal sheath about his stalwart cock.

Whatever the inspiration, I can chronicle only that their second joust lasted well over a quarter of an hour, during which time his black-haired consort achieved her climax at least three times before he finally spewed forth his copious libation into her devouring, voracious matrix.

I had had a long journey and I had seen much of the customs of this new land. It was time for me to seek my repose, awaiting the famous grape-treading contest of the morrow. I had a notion that somehow I might intervene and thus, in my infinitesimal way, determine the outcome of that contest. However, just before Guillaume and Margot prepared to renew their amorous frenzy for the third time that night, the worthy wine-maker grumbled, "But there is one element of this contest which pleases me not, beloved Margot, wife of my bosom."

"What is that, pray tell?"

"Why, as you know well, it is the tradition of this village that the patron himself will bed the winner at each harvest time. Now I like not the thought that this scrawny, wizened, rich and boastful old fool shall have the right to gaze upon your naked treasures and to enfold them in his bony arms. But that is what will happen if you are the winner tomorrow."

"Oh, Guillaume, how little you know after these many years of marriage," Margot lovingly whispered as she bent her head to deposit a tender kiss upon his limp cock. She began to fondle it between her palms until it showed signs of restoration, and then she added, "I know the tradition as well as you, but a woman has ways of seeming to yield to an importunate lover which will excite him and defeat his purpose. I give you my word of honor as your faithful wife that if I am brought to bed with Monsieur Claude Villiers, not one drop of his aged spunk shall reach my matrix. I will so disport myself with him that, I warrant you, his seed will spurt on the ground before his prick comes within a yard of the little cleft which is reserved for your mighty tool."

This speech so enflamed the good Guillaume Noirceau that he rolled over onto his back and pulling his naked, comely wife over on top of him, let her mount him and take the initiative, so that he might fondle her dangling pear-breasts and pinch and smack her wriggling backside as she arched up and down on his rigid prick. I was amused at this happy solution to their hypothetical problem, and so I left her tresses to perch on the top of the dresser opposite the bed so that I might take my well-earned repose and be on hand at the harvest-time festival, ready to intervene as I saw fit and thus, in my imaginative Flea's way, alter the destiny of mankind, and, of course, womankind as well.

CHAPTER FIVE

As early as dawn of that next morning, it was evident that the day of the grape-treading contest would be serenely beautiful so far as the elements were concerned. There was no wind, the sun was warm even as it climbed in its early journey over the heavens, and the radiant blue sky looked down upon the little village of Languecuisse.

As for myself, I looked down from my little corner of repose to regard Dame Margot and her worthy benedict, Guillaume, wrapped in each other's arms. The sheets were awry and rumpled and profusely stained with their many offerings to Venus and Priapus the night before. It was evident that both of them were lusty lovers and that Dame Margot was sufficiently endowed with energy and zeal to give a good accounting of herself in the wine vat just as she had done in the bed of love. She had been amply fucked many times that night, returning to each bout with the same frenzy she had taken to the first. Her cunt was hungry for cock, without a doubt.

I decided to attend the festival and to examine the contestants before deciding what role I should play.

After having listened to the conversation of Lucille and Margot and their husbands, I was not too greatly concerned with their boasting or their wagers. Both couples had a sanguine outlook which would prevent dire deeds of dark jealousy should one or the other persuade the other wife or husband to transfer, temporarily of course, carnal allegiance. Between Lucille and Margot, there was no particular reason why I should choose to befriend one over the other.

What interested me far more was this Laurette Boischamp, whom Jacques Tremoulier had praised as an exemplary paragon of beauty and all the feminine virtues. If, as I had heard, this exquisite damsel was fated to wed a doddering old fool, then perhaps it was best that I intervene on her behalf to protect her tender maidenhood from the ravages and despoilment by this detestable Monsieur Claude Villiers.

I left the cottage and moved about the little village, familiarizing myself with it and at the same time enjoying the warm French sun. By noontime, the crowd was already gathering just outside the long, low edifice where the grapes were stored and ultimately bottled. This establishment was owned by the same Monsieur Villiers.

The foreman of the vineyard, who was a sort of overseer—a burly brute of a man with beetling eyebrows, a massive chin and beady, suspicious little eyes—was ringing a cowbell to summon all the workers to enjoy a lunch of bread, cheese, and wine furnished for them by their estimable and charitable patron himself. There were tables and benches, and some of the wives of the villagers acted as cupbearers, moving about with jugs of wine and filling the cups of those who sprawled on the benches ogling them. I saw many a hand reach out shyly under a skirt or into a blouse during this festivity, and it spoke well for the ardent temperament of these villagers of Provence.

The warm sun and the good wine and the generous exposures of tempting female flesh began to evoke a kind of bucolic orgy. Several of the couples, after they had eaten and drunk their fill, crept away from the benches and made their way either to a large barn to one side of the storage building or boldly went into the hedges surrounding the first vineyard, where they fell on each other without more ado and coupled heartily and swiftly. And then, their tensions thus immediately alleviated, they rearranged their rumpled clothing and made their way back to the benches to await the principal ceremony.

At about two in the afternoon the foreman, whose name I had learned was Hercule Partrille, rang the bell once more to summon the attention of all the contestants and spectators. He announced in a bellowing voice which could have been heard a league away, that the excellent Monsieur Villiers would speak to them all to open the contest and give it his blessing.

I had found myself a place of concealment near a discarded and emptied bottle of wine near the little platform on which this brawny overseer stood to address his subordinates. When I beheld the patron my sympathies were immediately with Laurette, though I had not yet laid eyes upon her. He was easily sixty if he was a day, he was nearly bald, with a circular fringe of white hair about his bony skull that gave him a most repulsive look, and his face was cunning and without the least redeeming quality of compassion or good fellowship so far as I could tell. A sharp pointed nose, thin ascetic lips, watery blue eyes that peered suspiciously at his workers as if begrudging this brief charity of dispensing food and wine as well as working time to such a gathering at the cost of his own cashbox. In a word, Monsieur Claude Villiers was not the kind of lover whom maidens would ever thank the Lord for in their prayers; they would be more likely to lament their misfortune at having to bed him.

His voice was reedy and cracked like a broken flute as he mounted the platform, surveyed his menials with a frosty smile, and bade them welcome to the annual harvest of the good grapes of Languecuisse. "I now declare the contest open, and I wish all of you bonne chance!" he concluded. "To the winner, as has already been announced, will go a dozen bottles of my finest wine as well as a month of free rental on the cottage in which she is fortunate enough to dwell."

"The old fool," murmured a handsome, brown-haired matron who sat at the end of the bench nearest the bottle on which I perched. "He does not mention that he expects to fuck her whose comely feet press out the most wine from the grapes in her vat. If he did, I have no doubt only the greediest of wives would enter such a competition, for bedding with M'sieur Villiers would be worth much more than a month of free rental. It would be an ordeal in itself to make such a withered prick stand at attention, mark my words."

"Have you not heard, Dame Caroline?" her neighbor across the table, a stout, pleasant-faced beldame with graying black hair but yet voluptuous curves of bosom and haunch, countered. "It is certain to be the fair Laurette, because that old fool intends to wed her. He has told Hercule to put fewer grapes into Laurette's cask than in those of all the others. Doubtless he wishes to sample his prize in advance and also accustom the unfortunate wench to her future duties."

The matron called Caroline threw back her head and laughed, revealing strong white teeth. "Then I would say that M'amselle Laurette should implore her dear maman to instruct her in the art of milking a man's prick with her lips, since assuredly that old boar, randy though he may be, will never be able to manage sufficient strength to thrust it into her cunt."

"Especially if, as I am certain, she still retains her hymen," was the laughing retort.

Now everyone was in a pleasant mood and awaited the contest. There were fifteen contestants in all, including good Dame Lucille and Dame Margot.

The stamping grounds, to speak literally, were placed at the eastern side of a long, low platform so that the contestants would not have the disadvantage of having the sun in their eyes. On the platform stood fifteen large wide wooden casks, broader than ordinary barrels, each with its own spigot and funnel through which would flow the pressings of the purple, red, and green grapes. The platform was raised about two feet from the ground, and just in front of and under the platform were fifteen stone vats into which the liquid pressings from the casks would fall. Thus the judge—who would naturally be the patron himself—might walk along and observe immediately the success or failure of each contestant.

The damsels and matrons who were to take part stood off to one side while the burly foreman assigned them to their proper casks, each of which had been numbered with red paint. Dame Margot drew the very first and Dame Lucille the second.

I watched with interest the glowering Hercule. Because of his fearsome size and scowling face, his position as overseer undoubtedly gleaned him not only increased labor in the vineyard, but also, no doubt, enforced surrender to his virile cock whenever his passion demanded respite between the warm suntanned thighs of these handsome matrons. He was of the bullying sort, the kind who might accuse an industrious female worker of not having picked her quota of grapes and threaten her with dismissal or a stoppage of her wages, unless of course, she was willing to give him compensation from her moist cunny. And when I espied the way in which he would help the contestant to clamber into her cask while cupping a breast or squeezing a buttock or even boldly passing his hand down over her crotch under pretext of assisting her in hoisting up her skirts, I vowed to bite him where he would feel it and so take his lecherous mind off the doubtless orgiastic thoughts teeming in his brutal brain.

At last came Laurette, who was to be in the fifteenth cask. I noticed, however, that he took her by the hand and led her as a gallant might lead a marchioness through the first measures of the waltz at a festive ball. He tried none of his tricks with her, I warrant you.

All of the contestants showed off their flesh generously to the warm sun. All wore skirts of white cotton that lowered just to the edges of their knees, and their blouses bared the shoulders and were yawningly cut to let the spectators feast their eyes on their favorite fruits of the vine, whether they be round or pear-shaped or apple-like or melon- and cantaloupe-contoured juicy fruits of love. If one could foretell by the ardent glances alone from the males who watched avidly from their benches, nine months hence those love-fruits would most likely be giving suck in the little village of Languecuisse.

But now I was caught up in my first good look at the beautiful young Laurette Boischamp. All that had been said about the damsel scarcely did her justice. She had soft white skin which was entrancing to the sight; and where the sun had justly kissed her bare arms and shoulders, a golden tan showed satiny soft and enticing. Her smooth and gleaming flesh was in the full bloom of her nineteen summers. Her hair fell in two thick plaits almost to her waist, golden and thick and lustrous. She wore the short white muslin skirt and low-cut blouse, and, like the others, her feet were bare. They were chiseled, dainty little feet, seemingly much too fragile for such vigorous work. One could better imagine them stepping daintily towards the nuptial couch in preparation for a good fucking rather than crushing the juice-laden grapes.

Once all of the contestants were ensconced

inside their casks, Hercule took hold of the cowbell
and shook it as a signal. Whereupon all the damsels
and matrons promptly hoisted their skirts to their
waists and pinned them up out of the way. A roar of
admiration went up from the male spectators on the
benches at the rapturous vision thus granted them. For
at least six of the contestants wore no undergarments,
so that the furry thatch between their supple, flexing
thighs boldly appeared.

Laurette, however, as befitted a maiden of her
tender years, wore dainty pink cotton drawers. Yet
they fitted her so snugly as to be virtually a second
skin, molding out the beautifully plump, closely set
cheeks of her behind, and evincing an exquisitely tasty,
plump mount of Venus in front.

The patron himself deigned to stare longingly at
Laurette, who promptly flushed and hid her charming
heart-shaped face in the crook of one beautiful bare
arm. Her eyes were wide, well spaced apart, of a sky-
blue hue in which any man might lose himself. She had
the most exquisite little nose with just a hint of
upturned tilt to it. Add to this a pair of full, ripe red
lips meant for kissing or for engaging the head of a
vigorous prick, and I trust that no lusty male in all the
world could ask for a more beauteous or winsome a
sweetheart. Even I, a humble Flea, could understand
the desire that a man could feel for such a wench.

Now that everything was in readiness, I could
see also that the charming contestants stood in the
cask up to their lower thighs, since grapes filled the
casks and rendered the height at which they were
presented to the spectators. There was an hourglass at
the edge of the platform, which Monsieur Villiers now
took up in his bony hand, and Hercule promptly
announced that the competition would last precisely
for one hour. At the end of that time, she whose vat
was most filled would bear off the prize.

Now, of course, as the contest would proceed, and the level of the grapes would be lowered, the luscious bodies of the females competing for the supposed honor would be less and less revealed. Perhaps this is why from the outset the bolder ones decided to present themselves without undergarments for the occasion. I caught sight of many a man winking and making gestures to this or that female in her cask, evidently with the idea of arranging some sort of copulatory assignation with her when the evening shadows fell.

The hourglass was reversed, Hercule rang the bell thunderously again, and amid the cries and exhortations of the spectators, the contest began.

Now I observed that there was some truth to the rumor I had heard that the elderly vintner had contrived to give Laurette a more facile task by putting fewer grapes into her cask, since at the very outset I could see her body exposed only to about her hips, where in all the other casks the loins—whether bare or bedrawered—were plainly visible.

It was an amusing spectacle, nonetheless. Margot and Lucille faced each other, their eyes sparkling, their fine bosoms heaving passionately as they put their hands on their hips and began to tread, their naked legs splashing up and down like pistons, trampling the soft pulp beneath, the liquid down into the vats below. They started at a merry clip so that their bosoms jiggled lasciviously as did their bottoms and their fine thighs. Such a sight naturally encouraged the eager male spectators to call out encouragements, many of which, I fear, were too salacious to permit inscription here. The consensus of these, however, was that every male who watched would have gladly given a month's pay to be mounted between the thighs of either Lucille or Margot, and promised each of them in turn so vigorous a fucking as to leave them bedridden for a week at least and of no use to their natural husbands.

Jacques and Guillaume, sitting side by side on a bench which faced that side of the platform where their wives toiled, shouted quips and ribald advice to their spouses, so I concluded that even without my aid or without the victory of either of those handsome trollops, it would not be long before the husbands would be sampling the forbidden delights of the other's wife without the least acrimony.

After deciding what was to be the end of that friendly rivalry, I felt myself free to devote all my attentions to the beautiful Laurette, and by thus doing, although I could not of course know it at the time, I altered my own destiny. Laurette did not face the crowd, but turned to one side and kept her eyes on the heavens, as if to render herself impervious to the lewd catcalls of the ardent men of Languecuisse. Her beautiful bare thighs flexed and tremored as her legs moved up and down with a measured gait. So did the sweet rounds of her bosom, which I was sure were unconfined beneath her low-cut blouse.

The wench who was in cask Number Nine was one of those who had not seen fit to cloak her loins in drawers. She was about twenty-eight, I would say, with thick, chestnut hair that fell in a voluptuous cascade to her hips. She was Amazonian, at least five feet, nine inches in height, with a magnificent pair of big, muskmelon-like breasts set close together in the thin and widely dipping stuff of her blouse. Her waist was surprisingly slim, but her haunches flared and her bottom cheeks were spacious rondures which jiggled tantalizingly each time her legs moved up and down in the assiduous work of crushing the grapes beneath her naked feet. Her name was Desirée, which means "Desired," and it fitted her like a glove. From the conversation which I overheard, I was informed that she was a widow, her spouse having died of a heart attack at the last harvest time. It was said also that his death was caused by an excess of carnal passion while riding between her thighs. It was said as well that it was a beautiful way to die.

There were several men there who shouted out, "Eh, ma belle Desirée. I would gladly wed you tonight if you would but promise that I could survive the night!" To which this bold jade called back without losing a step of her tread, "Pooh! You would not last long enough to take off your trousers, for the sight of my cunt would make you lose your juice before you could put your prick between my legs!"

I thought her most likely to emerge the victor because of her magnificent build and powerful legs. She had full, firm, round calves browned by the sun, and her thighs were of the same sunset tinting, rippling with muscles. But most dazzling of all was the thick mane of dark chestnut curls which entirely hid the plump mouth of her slit, and even old withered Monsieur Villiers stared greedily at that superb lodging place for a virile cock.

The sand in the hourglass continued to trickle and the contestants began to tire, for they could not keep up the relentless pace at which they had started. Dame Margot, being goodly of girth, was first to tire, and beads of sweat ran down her cheeks. From moment to moment she would catch the sides of her cask and hang her head and pant to regain her breath, then go back to her treading.

Lucille mocked her and declared, "You have pressed only half a liter! I will press more than that from your Jacques' prick tonight if you can do no better when the hour is up!"

At the edge of the crowd of spectators, many of whom were standing up to get a better view—for by now the grapes were lowered in the casks and the bodies of the fair participants were less visible than at the start—I could see a forlorn, but very handsome, blond youth wearing a shepherd's hat, a rough cloth coat, and patched trousers which badly needed replacement rather than mending. A heavy-set bald man seated at the last bench at the back, raised his wine glass, turned to the young fellow and guffawed, "Look your last upon fair Laurette, poor Pierre, bastard that you are! It will not be long before the banns are read in the church by Père Mourier."

The youth, the same age as Laurette, clenched his fist and half made to throw himself upon the fat gossip but restrained himself with an effort. He stared longingly at beautiful, golden-haired Laurette. So this was Pierre Larrieu, the unfortunate apprentice to the patron who owned the village and who would soon own Laurette's delicious titties and virgin cunt, and all her other charms. I confess a sympathy, though I am not usually one to play Cupid. But contrasting him to the withered, juiceless vintner, I felt that somehow he should be permitted to have his fill of beautiful Laurette, even if he could not hope to wed her.

Besides, it was in my Flea-ish nature to enjoy intrigue and plots and also to pay off this Monsieur Villiers in a way that would not cause his subjects, the villagers, to suffer. For if one of them had dared affront him, his reprisal would have been swift and merciless, whereas if I, an invisible, infinitesimal insect without thought or personality—for that is man's common concept of my species—were to pay him off, he could blame no one.

At last the hour had run out and Hercule sounded the cowbell a last time.

The spectators sat back on their benches while their women passed among them pouring out more wine to drink the health of all the contestants and then that of the noble patron himself—which last was a waste of good wine, indeed. He, meanwhile, nursing a bony chin with an equally bony hand, passed slowly along the platform, not without casting many a covert glance upwards—especially at those wenches who had been shameless enough to bare their cunts. Finally he stopped at Laurette's vat, looking upwards and forced what passed for a beaming smile to his dry lips.

Then he turned to the crowd and announced in his reedy, dry voice, "I declare M'amselle Laurette Boischamp the winner, since from her vat came more wine than from any of the others. Hercule will lead her to my house this night to claim her prize."

There were jeers and hisses, but those who uttered them took care not let the patron catch them in the act. As for Margot and Lucille, they angrily burst out into a tirade, each accusing the other of coming out second best, and both calling upon their husbands to judge. Both those worthy men, after peering at the vats, come to the conclusion that it was Dame Margot who pressed more juice.

And so Guillaume helped Lucille down while Jacques, grinning from ear to ear, assisted Margot out of her cask and let his hands roam over her jouncy, oval bottom cheeks. Yes, I had no doubt that there would be a change of marital partners that very night.

As for far Laurette, it was the brawny overseer who, at the order of the patron, assisted her when it came time for her to emerge from her cask. He was most circumspect in handling her luscious charms, for though he was probably a terror with the women when left to his own devices and making full use of his authority, he could not risk offending his master.

Laurette blushed, her eyes downcast, sensing what awaited her at the patron's house this night. Her parents came forward to congratulate her. Her father was a thin man with spectacles, who looked like a cleric and her mother was stout and something of a virago. No doubt it was the latter's insistence that had compelled poor Laurette to accept so meager a husband.

CHAPTER SIX

The roistering had died away and the sun had set on the little village of Languecuisse. I had made my way, at the conclusion of the grape-treading contest, to the humble cottage of Laurette's parents, where I crept unnoticed into the bedchamber of the fair damsel and positioned myself upon the thin pillow where she was wont to lay her golden head at night—alone. This night was to change such circumstances. Yet you would have thought, seeing her so mournful while her mother fretted about her, that she was being prepared for execution on the guillotine. There were tears in those cerulean-blue eyes which crept down the soft round cheeks of the sweet, innocent face. The full red lips trembled with woe, as her mother chided her in a most officious contralto voice, "Do stand still, Laurette! Ventre Saint-Gris! M'sieu Villiers will grumble if he sees your eyes red from weeping. Why, girl, it is an honor which every maiden in Languecuisse envies you this night. Imagine! To be invited to the house of the patron himself, and just think that you have won a full month of rent on our home for your industrious work in the cask this afternoon. And just think of those bottles of wine! How your dear father and I will enjoy them!"

"That is all very well, Maman," Laurette sighed in as sweet and languorous a voice as I have ever heard from a maiden, "but you know very well that I detest M'sieu Villiers and I do not want to be his wife at all."

"You exasperating minx, take care lest I box your ears!" the mother cried in great anger. "Père Mourier is to read the banns from his pulpit after high mass next Sunday, as you well know, and you will be wed ten days later in the good church. Your poor father and I are overcome with joy to see your ascent from the poor and downcast to the most exalted. Why, think, child! You will be rich! You will have beautiful gowns to wear, jewels, the finest of food. You may even journey to Paris, which your father and I have never seen and never shall because we are too poor. And you complain, ungrateful girl!"

"But all those joys are for you and Father," Laurette entreated sorrowfully, "for it is I who will have to share M'sieu Villier's bed, not you."

Her mother slapped Laurette's soft cheek drawing a piteous cry from the unhappy maiden. "You impertinent baggage! You are not yet too old to taste the strap on your naked bottom, girl, so cease this wailing and stupidity at once, or I shall have your father attend to you this moment! And then how will it look when you go to the house of the patron with an aching bottom under your finest skirt and drawers?"

"But I don't love him, Maman," Laurette again uselessly protested, wringing her hands in despair. "Didn't you love Papa when you married him?"

"It is the duty of a wife to attend her husband in all circumstances of sickness and health," her mother piously enjoined. "As to your father, I learned to love him after we were wed, and as a consequence you came from my womb. Tell yourself that you are fortunate in providing comfort for your parents in their old age after all the labor and the many sous they have expended upon you during your childhood. You have won redemption in the heavens for this good deed. As for love, bah—what is that? All men are alike in the dark between the sheets, as are all women. You will soon find this out, but I do not need to tell you your duties for Père Mourier, who is your confessor, will remind you with what obligations a young bride must be burdened when she accepts the holy state of matrimony. Yet by accepting them, Laurette, you are guaranteed a happy future. Come now, let me see you smile again. Things are not so bad. Old M'sieu Villiers will not live forever, and if you are discreet, there are ways of having your pleasure with another lover. But mind you do not disgrace your married name or bring shame upon your parents."

"But I want to marry Pierre," Laurette insisted, earning herself a slap on the other cheek which left roses amongst the lilies and drew yet another woeful cry.

"That no-account bastard! What future could you have with him, except to bring forth a parcel of brats into this cruel world?" her mother indignantly ranted. "It is simply by the goodness of his heart that the patron gives that miserable young wretch employment. He lollygags about, hardly does a good day's work, and I am told he spends his time trying to write sonnets to his lady loves. If ever I hear that your name appears in those sonnets, Laurette, bride though you may be of the good patron, I shall bid him thrash you well for sullying our good name and his. Now, get a bit of powder on your cheeks. I have some rice powder, saved from my own wedding years ago that will do well for this occasion. And then Hercule will escort you to the patron's house."

But at this moment, as happy fortune would have it, there was a knock on the door of the Boischamp cottage, and, when Laurette's mother opened it, she found a little boy who brought tidings from the patron himself. It appeared that the overseer had been taken ill of a sudden and was confined to his bed, and therefore the charming M'amselle Laurette would go unattended to the house of the patron at her earliest convenience so that he might accord to her the prize she had so gloriously earned this afternoon. The frown on the face of Laurette's mother showed that this news was not especially welcome. She had hoped for the greater honor of her daughter being escorted by the overseer himself. But since this was not possible it was important only that Laurette reach the patron's house so that the ceremonial and prize might be accorded her, this being the first real step towards the eventual marriage on which she had set all her mercenary hopes. She therefore sharply instructed Laurette to waste no time in going across the field, but make straight for the house of the patron at the top of the hill, and there to be dutiful, obedient, and humbly grateful in all things. "And I wish you to mark well what I say—in all things, you obstinate minx. For the patron will doubtless report to me on the morrow of your behavior this night in his luxurious abode, and woe betide your naked bottom, Laurette, if the report does not do you justice. Now go and do not loiter!"

Laurette had been dressed in her prettiest gown, under which she wore a camisole and blue drawers, but her legs were deliciously bare and her dainty feet were shod in the rough shoes which were all that peasants could afford. She set forth valiantly across the rolling vineyards. Her parents sat themselves down to a celebratory feast of wine and sardines to congratulate themselves on the excellent match they had brought off for their beautiful, virginal daughter. They were too greedy in their anticipation of profiting from this ill-matched union to consider that their only daughter might encounter grave dangers as she went alone through the vineyard under the darkened sky. I decided to accompany her as a kind of guardian angel.

I had already determined that if she should be closeted with the senile patron and he should attempt to fuck her, I would prevent fruition of his perfidious scheme, at least until they were legally united. Remembering what I had read in history of the ancient custom of the droit de seigneur, I thought it likely that a man of his unsavory and lecherous character might attempt to pluck the flower and then send her back to her parents and say she was spoiled and not worthy of being his bride.

Laurette walked along slowly, head bowed, her slim little fingers clasped together as if in prayer. The wind was soft and gentle and it caressed the hem of her gown and the sweet white flesh of her ankles and lower calves. The moon shone down in all its radiance, and even the stars twinkled their admiration of this golden-haired virgin winding her way to the house of the lord and master of the village and towards a fate which, innocent though she doubtless was, she surely must suspect.

And then suddenly, as she turned the bend of one lofty, thick hedge of brambles which divided the vineyard of one farmer-tenant from the next, a shadowy figure rose and seized her. But, before she could cry out, he put his hand over her mouth and whispered, "Chérie, don't you know me? It's your Pierre!"

Laurette uttered a cry of joy and flung her beautifully rounded arms around her lover. They embraced lingeringly, and it was a tender, though passionate, kiss. In it I could see nothing that suggested that either of them was corrupt. "Where are you going by yourself in the dark, my dearest one?" Pierre murmured in a manly, resonant voice.

"You know very well, alas," Laurette uttered with a doleful sigh. "I have been summoned to the house of the patron to collect my prize. And worst of all, dear Pierre, a catastrophe has befallen me. My dear mother has just announced to me that Père Mourier will read the banns of my betrothal to the patron next Sunday. Oh, whatever shall I do? You know how I detest him! You know how he treats all the women who work in the fields. He pinches them, Pierre."

"Has he pinched you? If he has, I'll strangle him, I swear to you, Laurette."

"Sh-h-h! We must not be overheard. We have so little time. If we loiter, he will send again to my parents to see what is keeping me, and our secret will be discovered. Oh, Pierre, whatever shall I do?"

"If I had many francs, I would wed you myself and take you far from this wretched little hamlet," the youth stoutly declared. "But you know that I have nothing except the charity which the patron gives me. And I know also that I am his bastard son, though he will not recognize me. It is not right that he should wed you, Laurette, when we have pledged ourselves to each other ever since we were both thirteen."

"I know," she nodded sadly. "We always hoped and prayed that some miracle would happen so that we could be wed. And we have not even had joy of each other. And now, tonight, I am very much afraid he will demand his rights in advance before I am his wife. I loathe him. To think of his fingers pinching my naked flesh puts me in a fit of horror. Oh, if I am doomed to surrender to him, will you not, for the last time that we shall be able to meet before my marriage, teach me what love truly is, dear Pierre?"

"Do you really mean it, Laurette?" the youth gasped. Laurette nodded, then buried her blushing face against his chest. He uttered a cry of exultation. "Oh, darling, my darling one! Then come with me. There is a little knoll by a tree just off old Larochier's plot, and there we shall hide and I will teach you all I know of love, my beautiful Laurette!"

The knoll was indeed an ideal hiding place, in a little declension of the ground and comfortably guarded by a thick, towering oak tree whose branches were leafy and obscured the starlit sky as if compassionately wishing to grant these two young lovers their little time for solace and privacy. Pierre Larrieu tossed down his hat and then removed his coat and laid it on the thick greensward, a gesture as courtly as that of any knightly cavalier. "Lie down there, Laurette, and you will not stain your pretty gown from the grass," he urged. The sweet girl blushingly obeyed, turning her face to one side and hiding it in those soft little hands. He knelt down, his face taut with youthful excitement and passion as he gazed upon his lovely, virginal sweetheart. As she had settled herself, the hem of her gown lifted to show a pair of the most bewitchingly dimpled milky knees I have ever beheld. He bent down towards her, his fingers took hold of her deliciously rounded naked calves and fondled them, while his lips pressed a long and burning kiss on one of those adorable dimples. Laurette uttered a little cry of feigned apprehension in which, however, could be heard the full overtones of an exquisite eagerness for carnal knowledge: "Oh, Pierre, what are you doing?"

"You said I might teach you of love, my darling. If we have only this hour for the rest of all eternity, let me do as I wish for the first and last time." She could not gainsay so eloquent an argument.

So shyly, still hiding her face in those soft hands, she murmured tenderly, "I can deny you nothing this night. When I think that in a little time I am alone with that detestable old man who wishes to pinch my bottom and my breasts and every other part of me, I shall pretend that it is you there instead of him, dear, loyal, loving Pierre!"

I could see already that there was a suspicious bulge at the top of his patched, tattered trousers. It was understandable after so exciting a declaration from those virgin lips. Perhaps Pierre, who was accused of writing sonnets instead of doing his arduous chores, had unexpected inventiveness as a lover, but he was also conscious that there was a very little time. Moreover, I have no doubt, had he revealed all his lore of young love, he might have given Laurette the impression that he was a profligate instead of her devoted swain. Whatever the reason, he took hold of the hem of her gown and raised it to the waist, revealing a single lawn petticoat, which undoubtedly had also been provided by her mother, since the material was yellowed by age. Laurette uttered another little sigh, but did not move, having given him carte blanche to proceed. This he did without further delay. Up went the petticoat to join the rolled-up gown, and now the occasional ray of moonlight which filtered through the leafy branches of the great protective oak tree dappled the milky flesh of beautiful young Laurette, naked from her ankles to the hem of her tight drawers. He put his hands on her thighs and stroked them lovingly, until her muscles twitched and her bosom began to rise and fall in flurried response. "Oh, my darling, what are you going to do to me?" she whispered tremulously.

"I want to fuck you, Laurette. I want to put my cock into your sweet little virgin cunt. Please, let me do it. There will never be another time for us—you know that. From now on, you will have to endure the patron's cock, and you will mourn your Pierre because he is not there to comfort you and give you what your sweet cunt should have," he boldly told her.

"I am a virgin, as you know, dear Pierre," she murmured, still averting her face and shielding it with her hand, "but I have heard Papa and Mama talking when they thought I was asleep, and I know that fucking makes babies. The patron would not want to marry me if you gave me a baby, Pierre."

"Little innocent, if he is going to wed you within a fortnight, he can never know whose baby it is you carry in your belly," Pierre laughed. Already his fingers had begun to stray under the hem of Laurette's drawers, tickling her groin and the satiny soft flesh of her inner thighs, drawing little squeals of wriggling paroxysms from the delicious girl.

"That is true," she at last admitted as her head turned to the other side, although she still hid her face from him.

"Then let me take down your drawers and fuck you, Laurette. Look what I have for you, my darling," he panted as he opened his trousers and liberated his sturdy young cock. He had been circumcised, and the deep groove set off his vigorous young thick-veined shaft from the large, oblong tip of his weapon. Laurette at last dared to take her hands away from her eyes to stare at this phenomenon. Her eyes grew very large and her lips formed a little O.

"Mon dieu, my darling Pierre, I did not dream a man could be so big as that down there! And where are you going to put that monstrous object? Surely it will never go into my little silt."

"Let us find out whether it will or not, my dearest one," he urged hoarsely.

"Oh, I am so afraid—wait, wait, don't take my drawers off yet," Laurette gasped as his fingers had already begun to insert themselves under the hem. "What if the patron finds that I have lost my maidenhead? I will be spoiled for him and he will cast me aside. Then my father will thrash me with the strap and disown me. Would you want that to happen to your poor Laurette?"

"I tell you that the patron will not be able to

perform his marital duties, so old and dried-up is his cock. Two weeks ago, when he did not know I was watching, I peeked between the shutters in his bedroom and I saw him bedded with Desirée, the widow who is to be the new housekeeper for good Père Mourier. They were both naked and he was kneeling over her and she had both hands playing with his dwindled cock to rouse him to fuck her. I swear to you that it was useless until she finally took it between her lips. Even then he could not keep it hard long enough to get it between her legs, but dribbled off his seed into her mouth."

"Pierre Larrieu! You are wicked and sinful to tell me such lascivious things!" she gasped. But then, in the manner of all maidens who are curious about the particular and peculiar phenomenon of fucking, she breathed, "Do you mean that Desirée actually put her lips over the patron's th-thing?"

"I swear it on my hope of salvation, my dearest Laurette. And that is why I swear your maidenhead is in no danger. He can never learn whether it is there or not, because he will not be able to enter your sweet little cunt unless he does so with his fingers. Oh, Laurette, I am bursting for you! Please, let me fuck you! Besides, we are wasting too much time talking and the patron will be looking for you."

"Yes, that is true, Pierre dearest. Very well! I would much rather have you fuck me than M'sieu Villiers. For I love you so dearly that it grieves me to think that it will be the patron who will take off my drawers henceforth and not you."

With a cry of joy, the youth ripped off Laurette's drawers and exposed the soft, sweet mound of her cunt. The lovely little golden ringlets curled over the soft thick lips so protectively and lovingly that he was enchanted by them and let his fingertips play with the silken hairs. Meanwhile, Laurette had twisted her face to one side and covered it up with her hands, as if in this way she was not party to what was being done and hence in no way committing a mortal sin.

"Oh, Laurette, my beloved sweetheart," he gasped as he bent his head and applied a lingering kiss on the tangle of soft golden curls which shielded her virgin cunt. Laurette squealed and arched herself up instinctively, while at the same time she put up her knees and parted them to grant him access to her bower. Thus encouraged, Pierre Larrieu clasped her naked thighs with his ardent fingers, and deftly disengaging her drawers, cast the final veil aside. He then hoisted himself into her saddle, and at once brought the tip of his cock to bear against the furry mount of her love mound.

Laurette uttered a gasp, "Oh, gently, darling! I don't think it can get into me, it's so big!" She lifted up her arms to him, and the youth put his arms under her shoulders to support her as his hips fused with hers. She shivered exquisitely as she felt the tip of his cock nuzzle against the soft pink lips of her sweet maiden's cunt. I was nearby on a blade of grass, with full view of what was taking place, and I could not find it in my heart to disturb these young lovers, meeting thus upon so sorrowful an occasion.

Pierre crept forward a little, just engaging the tip of his weapon in the pouting lips of her crack, and Laurette again uttered a little squeal of mingled delight and fear. "Oh, Pierre, do it gently, I beg you. It tickles so nicely. Do not hurt me."

"Oh, my darling, I would never hurt you. Oh, how wonderful it is to fuck you, Laurette! Your thighs are so round and firm and white, you do not know how I have dreamed of doing this for so many years!" he declared.

Carefully he pushed forward a little more until the head of his prick was swallowed up just inside the lobbyway of Laurette's virgin orifice. She clung to him desperately and tenaciously at the same time, her eyes closed, her face scarlet with delicious blushes, awaiting the act which would make them one inseparably, no matter what should be the outcome.

"Now I must push it in a little harder, darling, and it may hurt just a little bit," he gallantly warned, as he steeled himself for the fray. "But once the pain is gone I promise you only unsurpassed joy. Oh, darling Laurette, how the lips of your cunt fairly kiss my cock, as if bidding it to go in all the way!"

"Oh, yes, I can feel them trembling about your thing," Laurette whispered shyly, convulsively digging her fingers into his shoulders. "Then fuck me, darling dear. Please, fuck me now!"

He drew a deep breath and then surged forward. At the same time Laurette, plagued by the vestigial fears which every virgin knows, even in moments of rapture, squirmed and tightened her thighs. The effect was to make him fall somewhat short of the mark of her hymen, although he undoubtedly must have banged against it, for she cried out, "Ai-i-i! I did feel a twinge then, darling. Oh, darling, I know it will hurt me, but I will be brave for your sake. Take me, fuck your little Laurette!"

"Who talks of fucking under the sky and the moon and the stars when the Creator Himself can look down and behold such wickedness?" there suddenly boomed a choleric voice.

Pierre Larrieu and Laurette Boischamp uttered a simultaneous cry of terror as the youth rolled off the half-naked, palpitating virgin. There, towering over them, stood the priest of the village, Père Mourier.

CHAPTER SEVEN

It was a tragi-comic scene, to say the least. There was the blond youth standing just away from Laurette, his tattered trousers about his heels and his hands clutched his turgid cock, his eyes bulging with mingled stupefaction and lust. There was golden-haired Laurette, sprawled on the greensward, her drawers lying near her naked thighs, her skirt and petticoat rolled up to her waist, her head raised up and her sweet blue eyes enormously dilated whilst her trembling hands shielded her golden-ringed cunt. And there, burly arms on his hips in his black cassock and ecclesiastical hat, stood the glowering priest of the village, his mouth agape at the iniquitous spectacle upon which he had come.

"What devil's work is this?" he thundered irately. "Mon dieu! Is it truly the gentle virgin Laurette Boischamp whom I thus behold in the very act of surrendering herself carnally to this detestable young fornicator?"

At this denunciation, Laurette began to sob pitifully.

"What dreadful sin have you two committed?" Père Mourier continued. He was short of stature and somewhat obese. He was possibly forty-five years of age, and his face was florid and his jowls were loose and flabby. His mouth was small but excessively fleshy, and his nose was bulbous. He was nearly bald, except for the sparse thatch of short gray hair which covered the rear of his skull and left his enormously broad forehead extending forward, thus giving him the look of a feared inquisitor. His eyes, surprisingly soft and brown as a woman's, were closely set together under gray, shaggy brows.

"Clothe yourselves quickly and let me see no more of this abomination," he went on. "You, Pierre Larrieu, you would dare defile this virgin out of wedlock? She is the betrothed of good Monsieur Claude Villiers. Next Sunday I am to pronounce their banns from my pulpit. And yet you would steal from that worthy humanitarian, who befriends all the villagers, that which is his sacred right!"

"Forgive me, Père Mourier," Laurette petitioned in a trembling little voice as she groped for her drawers and, modestly turning herself so that her back faced the angry priest, swiftly pulled them up over her thighs and loins, once more veiling her maiden crotch. "It was my fault, mine was the sin. Punish me, but do not harm my darling Pierre! If I could, I would wed him a thousand times, poor though he be, rather than the patron!"

"Child, child," the priest interposed almost cajolingly. "You are too young and innocent to know whereof you speak. Monsieur Villiers is an honorable man, and he has given much to the Holy Church. He has given work and good wages and lodging to all the inhabitants of Languecuisse. To wed with him sanctifies you. Thinking of marrying this boy, whose lineage is spurious, is out of the question. He does not even work as a tenant farmer under the patron, so how then could he support a family? It is unthinkable that the two of you should commit such licentious wickedness."

By this time Laurette had rolled down her petticoat and skirt. She then slowly rose to her feet, steadying her back against the huge oak tree, her face scarlet with sweet confusion. Her young lover, who had just failed to obtain his objective between her snowy thighs, had tugged his trousers back on and sheepishly hung his head as the good father excoriated them.

"Were you not sent for this night, my little one, to go to the house of the patron to receive your deserved reward for your triumph in the festival this afternoon?" the priest gently questioned.

"Oui, mon père," quavered Laurette.

"And yet you tarried that you might have a sinful rendezvous with this good-for-nothing," Père Mourier went on, his jowls quivering with indignation.

"No, mon père," the youth valiantly interposed. "It was I who waited here in the fields and waylaid her. I told her that once she wed the patron our joy was done forever and I implored her to yield to me just once. That is heaven's own truth, mon père!"

"Well, well, well, I do not know what to believe. What I saw with my own eyes told me only that both of you were about to a commit mortal sin. But answer me on your hope of salvation in the next world, Pierre Larrieu: did you take her maidenhead just now?"

"Oh, no, mon père," the youth blurted, his own face reddening with shame at the reminder of his failure.

"Well, at least that is something," the priest conceded. "But both of you must be punished nonetheless. Pierre Larrieu, you will get you to your hovel at once, and before you seek repose you will say a hundred Pater Nosters. And you will pray for divine forgiveness. You will not dare to lift your eyes to another virgin in this village or I shall tell the patron and have him banish you from Languecuisse. Do you understand me?"

"Yes, mon père," the youth groaned.

"Then go!" the priest commanded, shaking his fist in the direction of the sky.

Pierre Larrieu hesitated a moment, reluctant to leave his sweetheart to the mercy of this fat ogre, for such he must have appeared to the passionate young lover who had been at the very gate of paradise only to be denied entry. "You—you won't punish Laurette too hard, mon père?" he faltered.

"I am the spiritual leader of this village, my son," Père Mourier sanctimoniously observed, "and I am responsible for the soul of Laurette as much as for yours. Yet, knowing her to be an innocent maiden and susceptible to the flattery of such rogues as yourself, I will temper justice with leniency, chastisement with forgiveness. Go now, before I tell the patron how you nearly stole his bride from him this night!"

Pierre Larrieu bade a wistful adieu to his blushing, embarrassed sweetheart, and then strode back towards the village. The priest waited until the sound of his footsteps had died away and then turned to Laurette: "My child, the devil himself lurks in darkness to lead astray the faithful. But we must drive the devil out. By rights, I should tell the patron what I saw just now. No, do not speak!" and he held up a warning hand as Laurette opened her lovely red lips. "You must humble yourself, my child. I will forgive your transgression if you submit humbly and docilely to chastisement. If you do this, I will know that you act in good faith. I will have word sent to Monsieur Villiers that you were taken ill this night and could not appear before him to accept your prize. Then of course I shall pronounce the banns, and within a fortnight you two will be man and wife. Then no sin will have been committed, and your transgression will have been pardoned, since you will have won redeeming grace by your submission to your spiritual confessor. Do you submit yourself, my daughter?"

Poor Laurette gave a disconsolate little sigh and nodded. Doubtless she thought to herself that even a session with this dour holy man was infinitely preferable to being alone with the obnoxious patron. Père Mourier bestowed upon her a smile such as he reserved for a fallen angel who had returned to the fold. "Then come along, my daughter," he obsequiously urged, and took hold of her wrist to ensure her compliance.

I quickly hopped to a fold of her skirt, curious to witness what would befall her. I wondered whether she would be escaping the fire only to fall into the frying pan, as it were. Had this been London, I would have been sure of it, but I did not yet know the habits of this portly holy man. En route to his ecclesiastical abode, Père Mourier adopted a gentler tone of voice—though it was still sonorous—in an attempt to put Laurette at her ease: "Come now, my child, do not look so sorrowful. Since you are still chaste, your estate is not damaged in the eyes of our worthy patron, who has given me to understand that he adores you and fumes with impatience to make you his lawful consort. To be sure, my daughter, you must pay the penalty for your weakness in having even considered such lubricity with Pierre Larrieu. You will confess to me exactly what you did, my poor misguided child, and then I shall decide what chastisement best befits your conduct. Once having sustained this with fortitude and humility, you will be in a state of grace and I shall make your apologies to the patron for having been unable to attend his summons."

"Oui, mon père," Laurette murmured, hanging her fair head and uttering yet another sigh of lamentation, doubtless at the thought of what she had missed with her young lover.

The little church with its towering steeple was

situated about a quarter of a mile west of the vineyards, and beside it was the rectory, which quartered the good father. He took hold of the knocker and struck it three times on the door, whereupon, after not quite a minute of waiting, it was opened by no less than the handsome widow Desirée.

"Good evening, Madame Desirée," the portly priest beamed. "As you see, I have returned with the prodigal lamb. May I entreat your indulgence to perform an errand for me?" Then, turning to the startled, golden-haired maiden beside him, the obese holy man gently added, "Madame Desirée was gracious enough to accept the post of housekeeper to me, since I am an impossible cook and have no time for tasks of domesticity because I must constantly look after my little flock."

"Oh," was all that Laurette could find to say. But then, glancing in wonder at the beautiful, chestnut-haired Amazon, she naively inquired, "But I thought—"

"Yes, my child, it happened this very afternoon. Madame Desirée is a widow, as you know, and there are many temptations lurking in this village where passions are hot and the blood is warm, thanks to the sun and the good grapes. So for her own salvation, she was happy to accept the post I tendered her. As for myself, I am indeed fortunate to have found so capable and so devout an assistant who will rid me of the burden of the small, irritating chores so that I may have more time to drive out sinfulness from Languecuisse."

After this long-winded introduction, he asked the Amazon to dispatch herself at once to the house of Monsieur Claude Villiers to inform that worthy patron that dear Laurette had been afflicted with a small seizure and conveyed her most humble apologies for being unable to present herself to him that night. Père

Mourier had Desirée add that Laurette was recovering and that she looked forward to the next Sunday when her name would be announced from the pulpit as the intended consort of so noble and charitable a man. And finally, he declared that, when Desirée had performed her errand, for which he gave her goodly thanks, she might go promptly to bed.

The handsome Amazon eyed Laurette rather scornfully, as if appraising her and comparing the virgin's charms with her own, which, as I have already related, were certainly considerable and splendidly proportioned. Then, after having procured a shawl against the possible chilly gusts, she set off across the vineyards for the abode of the patron. Père Mourier, resuming his hold of Laurette's wrist, led her inside his dwelling and thence to his very bedchamber. Here, having surreptitiously bolted the door, he turned to her and bade her go down upon her knees and clasp her hands and bow her head for her confessional.

"Now then, my daughter," he began, "open your heart and do not be afraid to confess your sinful thoughts as well as deeds. A good confession is half the battle towards redemption of the sinner. Never forget this."

"I will remember it, my father," Laurette meekly returned.

"Now, answer me truthfully. You are certain that this rogue did not deflower you? I know that you are still a tender maiden, dear Laurette, but since you are intended for your nuptials within a fortnight, surely your worthy parents must have given you some inkling of the duties which fall upon you as the bride of the patron. You understand, then, what I mean?"

Laurette's fair, milky cheeks turned a vivid crimson as she nodded. Drawing a deep breath, and keeping her eyes modestly lowered, she faintly replied, "H-he didn't do it to me, my father."

"But he was about to, was he not?"

Another nod and a heartfelt little sigh. Doubtless once again poor Laurette was remembering the forbidden moment of near-ecstasy, which the worthy priest had so unexpectedly halted.

"But did you not struggle and resist this ravisher?" he sternly resumed his interrogation.

"N-no, my father. I-I love him so and it was to be the last time we met before—before—"

"Before you took your vows of matrimony, I daresay. Well, my daughter, as a compassionate man who understands the foibles of his brothers, I can perhaps understand your weakness. But surely you could not think of wedding Pierre Larrieu. And to give yourself to a man out of wedlock is surely sinful, this you know from all my teaching and that of your good parents, do you not?"

Laurette's golden head dropped even more as she whispered an affirmative.

"Now, if he had forced you against your will and if you had cried out for help, my daughter," the obese priest pursued, "the sin would not have been yours. Am I to understand that you allowed him to unclothe your private parts so shamefully? When I came upon you, my child, I blanched with horror to observe that your drawers were lying upon the grass beside you and that your petticoat and skirt were rolled up to your belly. Was this done by force, my daughter? Be truthful now!"

"I-it was not done by force, my father," Laurette quavered, and two big tears glistened in her large blue eyes.

"Alas, what you have just told me fills my heart with sorrow. For a pure maiden to permit such licentiousness is indeed reprehensible, my poor child. Do you give me your promise never to see this wretch again?"

"But, my father, I would do so, and yet what if through no fault of mine he appears before me?"

"Take care, my daughter," Père Mourier's shaggy brows knitted in a stern and foreboding look. "Do not try to entrap me in such devil's logic! Why, then, in that instance, you will modestly remember your station in life and the fact that you must not allow a blemish to stain the good Christian name of Claude Villiers. And you will tell this scoundrel that it is odious to you to be accosted by him. So much for that. And now, my daughter, the moment has come for your chastisement. Are you prepared to submit to it at my hand?"

Laurette, who was blushing from her temples to her milky throat, uttered a poignant sigh and nodded.

Removing his little hat of office, the portly priest moved now to a chest of drawers beside his narrow bed, opened the top drawer and drew out a scourge. It was made of brown leather with a short stocky handle from which dangled a thin thong about two feet long. At the last six inches of the thong, the leather had been split down the middle to form two tapering lashes, about a quarter-inch in thickness and as much in width. When he turned back to her, Laurette shrank back, eyes wide with fright, and clasped her soft little hands to her rosy mouth.

"Yes, my child," he said sorrowfully, "one drives out sin by chastising the very flesh where it has entered or sought to enter. I do this for your own salvation, my sweet daughter. Accept the scourge in true humility and reparation for your having yielded, even infatuated though you were, to the impure desires of this young scoundrel. Mayhap this punishment will also bring you to sober reflection upon the precepts you must follow to obtain a good and holy marriage."

"I—I will, my father," poor Laurette faltered.

"Excellent! Your docility and resignation restore in me the glad hope that redemption is still possible for your soul, my gentle Laurette. Now, I enjoin you to kneel upon that chair, to hoist your skirt and petticoat to your waist, and hold them there tightly while I proceed to inflict your well-merited punishment."

He made a gesture with the scourge toward a heavy, straight-backed chair near the window, whose shutters had already been drawn for the night. Poor Laurette slowly arose, and reluctantly approached the altar of her atonement. Slowly she knelt down upon the hard seat of the wooden chair, and, as she grasped the hems of her skirt and petticoat, I hopped upwards till I had reached the crown of her lovely head. Very slowly she drew up these protective garments till they were lodged about her waist, thus exposing her beautiful buttocks, snug in the tight thin drawers which she had already discarded once, such a little while ago and under such different circumstances.

The worthy priest now advanced, his eyes glistening with anticipation. Transferring the scourge to his left hand, he proceeded to insert the fingers of his other hand inside the waistband of Laurette's drawers. The poor girl uttered a cry of shame, and turned her scarlet face toward him in agonized appeal.

"Do not dismay, my daughter," he gently consoled her, while tightening his grasp of the waistband of her thin drawers, "this humiliation which you are about to feel is properly wholesome, since it at once indicates to me that all sense of modesty has not yet fled your gentle nature. If there is pain and shame in your punishment, my child, know that we must all suffer upon this earth, not only for our sins but also for those which we even consider."

"But—but, mon père," Laurette quavered, "c-can you not punish me without removing my drawers? They are very thin and they will not protect me very much from that awful whip."

"Alas, my child, it is simply vain pride which compels you to speak so to me, your confessor," Père Mourier sighed. "Moreover, we speak now of degrees of shame. If you felt naught at exposing your most intimate parts to that young scoundrel a moment ago, how can you argue against baring yourself to the disciplinary scourge which will drive out wickedness? Resign yourself, my daughter, for it is the custom of a father who thrashes his daughter, just as I, your spiritual father, am about to do, to administer it upon the naked flesh itself. Bow your head humbly and pray for redemption, dear Laurette."

The poor girl did not dare refuse and so with a stifled sob of apprehension and despair, bowed her head and submitted herself. With a greedy smile, the portly holy man tugged down her drawers till they rested just above her knees, thereby exposing the magnificent, milky white contours of her bare behind and splendidly rounded soft thighs. At this exposure, Laurette gasped and contracted all of her muscles in an instinctive defense which, of course, only served to accentuate her magnificently developed posterior. The cheeks of her bottom were marvelously rounded, with the most harmonious proportion of curves from waist to hips. They were set rather closely together, resembling the amber furrow which parted them, and their plump summits and the mouth-watering, swelling base of those luscious nether globes would have tempted a saint to risk perdition. I much doubt the Père Mourier was a saint, and I suspected that this means of chastisement was also a favorite penchant with him. For his florid face became still redder, and his eyes sparkled with an unholy joy, while the broad wings of his nostrils flared and shrank. Not only that: I perceived a sudden protuberance making itself known against his black cassock, just at the juncture of his thighs.

He did not at once begin the discipline. Instead, his thick, short hand lingeringly passed over the milky skin so innocently offered to his licentious view and touch.

Poor Laurette fidgeted about uneasily on her penitential chair during this greatly prolonged interlude. Her fingers convulsively twisted the upturned cloth of her gown and petticoat while the good father stood to one side surveying the bewitching nakedness which his golden-haired penitent so unwillingly revealed. Laurette's thighs were beautifully made, neither too plump nor too lean, swelling with gradual ripening above the knees till they merged with the plump roundness of her backside. Her lovely calves were also well worthy of admiration, as were the adorable, soft knee hollows. Père Mourier frowned and approached the chair as if dissatisfied with the position of his victim.

"Bend your head and shoulders over the back of the chair, my daughter," he instructed in a voice that thickened with lubricity. "Very good. Offer your sinful bottom to the corrective sting of the scourge. For this, too, is an act of humility which will not be forgotten. And now, move your knees a little more apart. Just so. I shall begin shortly, so steel yourself, my child."

He bent now and tugged her drawers down a little more, wishing to uncover as much of that milky flesh as possible, though he did not intend to scourge all of it. His eyes feasted on the trembling cheeks of her backside, which quivered and contracted relentlessly as her suspense was agonizingly continued.

Finally, placing his left palm on the small of her back so that he might have direct contact with her gleaming white skin, he raised the scourge and applied a rather gentle lash across the tops of her deliciously swelling hips. More startled by the unexpected contact than by pain, gentle Laurette uttered a little "Oh!" and her naked hips squirmed from side to side. Hardly the faintest pink mark showed on the milky flesh where the split thong had kissed it. By now the obese father's sexual weapon was ferociously extended, forcing out the thin black stuff of the cassock as if it intended to pierce it in its quest for freedom.

A second lash now followed, slightly lower down, the two tips of the lash whisking around towards Laurette's tender groin. Another "Oh!" escaped the lovely penitent, and she convulsively clenched her thighs and bottom cheeks. "No, no, my daughter," he said hoarsely. "Do not resist the discipline. Submit yourself completely, for that is the only way to escape perdition. Once more, stick out your backside and move your knees well apart."

"Oh, do please hurry and end it, mon père," Laurette whispered, her eyes tightly closed.

But this was a request that the good father had no intention of granting. In fact it seemed as if he delighted in this flagellatory penchant and attained his greatest satisfaction when the ordeal was endlessly prolonged by interruptions and sermons. There was, to be sure, practical wisdom in his method of application: The longer he kept poor Laurette kneeling on that straight-backed chair, the longer his glittering eyes could feast on the twisting, wriggling, flexing and contracting cheeks of her voluptuous and virginal behind, thus inflaming his carnal passions.

He took careful aim now and adroitly whisked the leather thong across the very center of Laurette's rotundities, so that the tips of the split end flicked towards her tender maiden crotch. The half-naked young virgin emitted a squeal of anguish, and her hips plunged this way and that, which made the cheeks of her delicious milky bottom jiggle in the most lascivious way. In turn, that sight caused Père Mourier's sexual organ to attain its maximum rigidity and length, and it was indeed formidable as it prodded out the stuff of the black silk cassock. Another lash followed, no more severely administered than the others, this one wrapping around the voluptuous base of her naked behind and drawing still another involuntary twist.

"Repent, my daughter," he said in a hoarse, trembling voice, "for the heat of the scourge will cleanse you. Verily, it will drive out those noxious tendencies to sinfulness which lurk within the very part of your body which I am castigating. Tell yourself, my poor child, that each stripe to your impudently jutting posterior is a step toward your eternal salvation."

Having delivered this oratory, the holy father dealt Laurette the next stroke a bit more sharply so that the tips of the leather thong flicked perniciously into her loins and very likely brushed the downy golden fleece of her virgin cunt. "Ahhrr! Oh, I am suffering, mon père!" she cried shrilly as her naked hips gyrated frantically. She turned back her tear-stained face appealingly to him. Noticing her hands clutching her upturned garments, he sternly bade her not to let them fall or greater severity in the treatment he was meting out to her would be her reward. Moving a little more to the left and farther away from her, but yet retaining his left palm on her naked lower back, he applied two or three quick strokes straight across the lower curves of her milky backside. These drew sobs and tears and new wriggling maneuvers which made his eyes blaze with sexual ferocity.

Yet actually the beating was not overly severe. True, there were faint pink streaks from the tops of her hips to her uppermost thighs, but there were no really cruel strokes to torture her. I thereupon concluded that this was a voluptuous flagellation, altogether ideal for bringing the blood to the surface of the pure soft skin and inflaming the penitent's subconscious ardors (for what purpose my readers and I can well guess).

"Oh, I implore you, mon père," Laurette cried tearfully as she shifted her beautiful bare knees on the hard wooden seat of her punishment chair, "I am not very brave and I cannot endure this much longer. Please, do finish it and pardon me, I beg of you!"

"Courage, my child, you have yet a good deal to suffer before your sins are purged," he retorted. "Would you bargain with the devil, then, for a lesser chastisement simply because your mortal flesh is weak and thereby lose your hope for heaven? Steel yourself and grit your teeth, Laurette. I am going to whip you very smartly now, my girl."

He was as good as his word. Now the leather flew through the air with more authority. He applied horizontal stripes all over Laurette's naked seat, while the unfortunate beauty sobbed and wailed and incessantly jerked her hips this way and that to evade the burning kisses of the lash. At one point, a particularly stinging cut across the base of her wriggling backside made her drop her clothes which promptly covered up the condemned area. But so engrossed was he in his good work of saving her soul that he did not chide her for this neglect, but instead with his own free hand he hoisted up her garments once again. But, not satisfied, he then dropped the scourge to the floor and sternly told her that he meant to lift her clothing so that it would not fall back again. Coming very close to her, he put his hands caressingly about her thighs and hips, fondling them a good deal, till at last he raised skirt and petticoat and dragged them up over her head and shoulders, letting them fall over her face to blindfold her and thus exposing her to her camisole, a kind of vest that descended to about the middle of her milky back. Slipping his thick hands into this delicate garment, he brushed past her firm young breasts, pushing the cloth aside. He loosened the silky ribbons that held the undergarment closed and pulled apart the two sides, leaving her charms exposed to his greedy view.

Telling her she might clutch the rungs of the chair in front of her to sustain herself, he retrieved the scourge and set about whipping her in earnest. Moving from side to side so as to command her entire bottom, he applied first a horizontal stroke, then a diagonal one, while poor Laurette, beside herself with pain and shame, cried out and twisted and jerked and wriggled in the most exciting manner.

"There," he said soothingly as he laid on a final stroke which wrapped the two split ends of the thong against her naked belly and drew a piercing cry from the unfortunate girl, "you have paid the price for your licentiousness, my girl, now kneel there in penitence and make your silent prayers to him who will be your lawful husband, that he will accept you to his bosom as a pure, untainted virgin. Meanwhile, I will soothe your hurts."

Casting aside the scourge, he approached the chair on which the half-naked, golden-haired virgin knelt weeping and squirming about. His pudgy hands, the backs of which were covered with thick black hairs, greedily but very lightly stroked and palpated her naked bottom. Laurette gasped at the very instant she first felt his profaning fingers take such audacious liberties, but she did not dare protest, fearing another application of the wicked scourge. Besides, her face covered by her petticoat and gown which he had pulled up over her, she could not see that he had rolled up his cassock to the waist, thereby exposing his obese, hairy, and massive maleness. For the cock of Père Mourier was really enormous; it surpassed in girth that of Guillaume Noirceau, and it was fully as long as that of Jacques Tremoulier. The head was a huge, obscene plum in size, with thick lips twitching as if impatient to disgorge its spew.

A fit of trembling overtook Laurette as she crouched on her whipping chair, compelled to suffer the holy father's attentions on her tender, streaked, and completely naked bottom cheeks. But after a bit she discovered that his fingers did not hurt her stripes but rather benevolently calmed the burning globes of her behind. Slowly she relaxed her vigilance and terror. Sobs still shook her lovely body, but they were muted now, delicious music to a flagellant's ears.

He crouched a little so that he might better examine the welts the scourge had left on those lovely hindquarters. Towards the end of the flogging, the tips of the lash had bitten against the inner edges of both bottom cheeks, and there were dark red little blotches visible. His fingers first lightly stroked these marks; then, very slyly and very slowly, he took hold of the lower curves of her behind and pried them asunder, disclosing the crinkly little rosebud of her virgin anus.

"Ohhh! Oh, what are you doing to me, mon père?" Laurette gasped, and the muscles of her bottom furiously tightened to hide this most intimate spot of all.

"My child, I am going to lave your hurts with some soothing oil. Do not be afraid. Surrender yourself, for this is a part of your penitence," he replied in a trembling, harsh voice, burdened by his overweening lust.

"I—I will submit," Laurette breathed, nearly swooning with shame. "But do please hurry and end my punishment, mon père. My bottom hurts so terribly and I am dying of shame to be like this before you."

"That very humiliation is part of the punishment," he sagely observed. "Now stick your bottom out a little more, my child. Ah, that is excellent! Now do not be alarmed and do not move until I tell you to."

Continuing his soothing strokes upon her virgin flesh with one hand, the father grasped his straining tool with the other. After a few jerks of his hand, his already tremendous pole grew even more, the veins standing out against the purple-hued flesh. The hand positioned on Laurette's backside slid lower down and worked between her firm thighs, soothing some of the streaks that had fallen there. As he rubbed up and down between her legs, the back of his hand brushed the curly hairs that stood sentinel around her cunthole. His cock jerked in repsonse to this close contact with that luscious orifice. He rubbed the full length of his ever stiffening flesh, holding back a groan as the sensations overtook him. Suddenly his hips thrust forward and he spewed his thick fluids over the backside of the unsuspecting girl. "Oh," she cried, "what have you splashed on me?"

Unable to respond to her innocent question immediately, he began rubbing the warm sperm over her startled bottom cheeks. "Just some soothing lotion, my child," he choked out, his voice not sounding quite right even to his own ears. He cleared his throat. "No need for the pain to continue now that you've had your punishment. Doesn't that feel nice, my dear?"

"Yes, Father," she said, somewhat surprised. "It's taken the burn right out." He let go of his only partially sated prick and continued rubbing her beautiful buttocks and thighs with both hands, spreading his spunk over her skin. Soon his stubby fingers were making ever smaller circles, moving in towards her puckered anus. His still-upstanding prick lifted higher again and he stepped forward. She clenched her buttocks involuntarily as she felt his fingers working the slippery liquid partway into her bottomhole. As she tightened, he grasped her flesh with both hands and spread wide her cheeks. One big stubby finger started easing into her tender inner bottom curves, distending her to the maximum. Before Laurette could cry out at the sharp twinge which this caused her sensitive anus, he had advanced the huge plum-head of his cock against the dainty, crinkly amber-pink rosette. The heat and firmness of that sear point made Laurette utter another cry and again contract her muscles, whereupon he angrily rebuked her: "If you do not stop this wriggling about until I bid you do so, my daughter, I shall be compelled to give you another beating. This time on the front of your thighs. I may even be forced to properly chastise the most sinful part of all, which you have merited by lying in the field with that miserable apprentice!"

With a heartrending sob, Laurette resigned herself. Once again, the obese priest prodded the tip of his savagely swollen cock against her nether orifice and was just about to engage it within the shrinking, tender hole when he was startled by a hammering at the door.

His face turned nearly purple with frustrated rage; for a moment he hesitated, but the hammering resumed. Muttering something under his breath, he unpinned his cassock quickly, and, frantically looking about, at last seized a hymnal which he held over the juncture of his thighs to conceal the impious swelling. Laurette uttered a cry of distress: "Oh, do not let anyone see me thus, mon père!"

He had gone halfway towards the door when her cry reminded him of the impropriety that might be exposed to alien eyes. Muttering something again, he hurried back to her, dragged down petticoat and skirt to conceal her naked bottom, and then whispered,

"Remain just as you are and do not say a word!"

Then, composing his florid, contorted features into a semblance of benign serenity, Père Mourier at last went to the door and opened it.

It was his Amazonian housekeeper Desirée, breathless, her face flushed and her eyes shining. He noted that the bodice of her blouse had been disarranged, exposing rather more of the valley of her sumptuous bosom than was proper in the rectory. But before he could remonstrate with her over this immodesty, she burst out: "Oh, mon père, I just came back from the patron. I told him about Laurette and he was grief stricken, but he bids you attend to her so that she will be well and in good spirits for the announcement of the banns. But, just as I entered, mon père, I was in time to admit a visitor who asked for you. He is Father Lawrence from London. Shall I show him in?"

"I will go to him in the little salon, Madame Desirée," Père Mourier said in a composed voice. "Will you do me the sweet favor of bringing wine and some of those little cakes you said you baked to celebrate your first day as my housekeeper? My guest will no doubt be thirsty and hungry, if he has come so far." And he gave the Amazonian beauty a fatherly pat on her opulent hip. His hand lingered a little longer than was absolutely necessary.

CHAPTER EIGHT

Père Mourier, now fully composed, entered the reception salon of the rectory to meet his mysterious guest. Meanwhile Desirée, hastened to procure a tray of cakes, two glasses, and a bottle of excellent Burgundy, which she set down on a table between the two priests. She did not at once withdraw, but stood at the doorway, making languishing eyes at the newcomer. He had evidently taken her fancy, for he was indeed a handsome and mature man in the full prime of his faculties. I suspected that it was he who had disarranged her blouse.

Father Lawrence was just under six feet tall, in his late forties, I should judge, with an abundant shock of brown hair only partly streaked with gray. He had vigorous, rugged features, intense blue eyes, thick brows, a strong roman nose, and a firm, decisive mouth and chin. He was so much more prepossessing than Père Mourier that I had no doubt the handsome widow was regretting her impulsive offer to become the latter's housekeeper just when a man of Father Lawrence's vitality and robustness appeared.

"I bid you welcome to the village of Languecuisse, Father," the obese holy man obsequiously greeted his confrère, extending his pudgy hand—the very one which had just dealt poor little Laurette such a thrashing on her naked behind (and also served to soothe her hurts in such a novel manner). "May I ask to what order you belong?"

"Why, to tell the truth, Père Mourier, it happens that a third cousin of my family resides in a town some fifty miles from your charming little village. I am in great need of a holiday so after my visit to my cousin I decided to see the rest of the countryside, particularly this area, which is so famous for its excellent wines."

"Indeed, Father, you have come to the right place for wines. This very day we held a grape-trampling contest to celebrate the harvest of the good grapes that make such delicious wine as this. Dear Madame Desirée, will you not do the honors?"

The handsome widow was only too happy to be called back to service in the presence of so virile and splendidly vital a visitor. As she opened the bottle and poured out the mellow red wine, her eyes fixed on Father Lawrence with an intense admiration while her superb enormous bosom swelled with ardor. He lifted his glass to toast the health of Père Mourier and laughingly declared: "To your health, my worthy colleague of France, and to the health of this attractive housekeeper. Now then, you asked me to what order I belong. I was about to say that after my holiday, I shall go to a new parish, having served faithfully my little flock in the Soho district of London. I have been assigned to the seminary of St. Thaddeus, and I am to return there in about a month. I look forward to my new duties, Père Mourier, but until that time I should much prefer to be treated like a visitor and to enjoy my leisure in this beautiful country of Provence."

He lifted his glass first to the obese holy man, and then towards Desirée herself, who modestly lowered her eyes and blushed properly, as a chaste widow should. Yet I remember how boldly she had exhibited her charms only that afternoon in the cask, when she had lofted her skirt and petticoat to expose herself without drawers.

Père Mourier fairly beamed at this news. "Why, then, Father Lawrence," he replied, "since that is your disposition, I, as spiritual leader of this pleasant little community, would like nothing better than to invite you to spend the rest of your holiday here. It is true that we do not have the excitement of the large cities, but we have many interesting sights and quite a few philosophical problems to occupy your alert mind, I am sure. As a matter of fact, just as I came to receive you, I was wrestling with the devil himself in seeking to drive him forth from a charming damsel who is without a doubt the most beautiful in our village."

The bushy eyebrows of the English ecclesiastic arched with interested surprise. "I should be most happy to accept your invitation. You know that the country I come from is but an island subject to fog and rain and cloudy weather. But here in beautiful Provence, I have already fallen in love with the sun and the green fields and the simple people of the earth. Of course, I should have to find accommodations somewhere." As he said this, he glanced artfully at the Amazonian housekeeper, who stood beside him, ready to fill his glass once again. Her red full lips curved in a comprehending smile, as she favored him with a sultry glance from under lowered lashes.

"That would be no problem," Père Mourier at once responded, "for I know a number of families who would be privileged to take you in as their guest."

"I should not like to be a burden on anyone. The ideal thing would be to find some little place and to engage a housekeeper, such as yours, for example, good Père Mourier."

The fat priest pursed his fleshy lips and furrowed his brow in concentration. "I know of one such place. It is a little cottage on the other side of the village, rather humble, and in it dwells an estimable widow by the name of Madame Hortense Bernard. I am certain that if I spoke to her she would be happy to put you up as a guest."

"Naturally, I should pay for my food and lodging," Father Lawrence smiled. "But tell me of this good soul. She is doubtless one of your parishioners?"

"Oh, to be sure," Père Mourier smiled with a knowing wink, for it was obvious that he felt already a certain bond of kinship between himself and the virile-looking English churchman. "She is the soul of devotion herself. She was bereaved two years ago when her husband fell into a vat of wine and was drowned. It was a dark night without stars or moon to guide the unfortunate man's footsteps, and it appeared that he had stumbled from a window, lost his balance and toppled down into the vat. Since then, Madame Bernard has grieved unceasingly for him. Indeed, had it not been for my good fortune in finding that Madame Desirée wished a situation, I should doubtless have engaged Madame Bernard. She has, you see, tenancy of a few acres of grapevines and the past two summers her neighbor's husband, the industrious Jules Dulac, has done a charitable work under heaven's eyes by looking after them for her. Yet unfortunately her soil was not blessed and thus the harvests have not been prosperous for her. She could very well use the francs you could pay her for your keep, good Father Lawrence."

"Then I should be indebted to you, Père Mourier, if you would, as is convenient, speak to this soul on my behalf."

"Consider it done. But meanwhile you will do me the honor of staying here for the night. In the morning, I shall go to Madame Bernard and make the arrangements. Madame Desirée?"

"Yes, Your Reverence," the beautiful Amazon cooed.

"I am certain that we can find a place for Father

Lawrence to sleep tonight. Will you see to it, my dear?"

"Nothing would give me greater pleasure, Your Reverence," Desirée purred, and with a glance she gave Father Lawrence to understand that the remark was really meant for him.

"So that is settled," the fat priest chuckled. "Now, Father Lawrence, perhaps you will lend me your spiritual aid in conversing with the fair penitent of whom I was speaking but a moment ago. Hers is a most distressing case, and I fear that because of her youth and innocence she is not yet resigned to her duty."

"I shall be most happy to collaborate with you, Père Mourier, in any way that you deem advisable," said the vigorous English ecclesiastic. Since Père Mourier was not looking at him at the moment he hazarded a glance at the chestnut-haired housekeeper, a look that told her he found her comely.

She flushed hotly beneath that gaze, and then volunteered, "If Your Reverence has no further need of me at the moment, I will prepare a bed for Father Lawrence."

"Do so indeed, my dear," Père Mourier beamed and gave a lordly flourish of his hand. "Come, Father Lawrence, and let us attend this charming penitent. I have only just finished with her discipline so that she may see the error of her ways."

Father Lawrence rose from the table and moved to follow his French colleague. But as Desirée had not yet left the room, he took stealthy advantage of her presence to pass his left hand quickly over her magnificent backside and to give it a most familiar little squeeze. She clamped a hand over her mouth to stifle a gasp of surprised delight, and then, flashing him an enamoured look from those magnificent eyes of hers, promptly left the room.

En route to the room in which he had left poor Laurette still kneeling on the straight-backed chair, Père Mourier swiftly explained the circumstances of her presence. Father Lawrence nursed his chin with a well-groomed hand and sighed, "Yes, I can see your problem, Père Mourier. This young person has already the devil's influence manifested by the young wretch whom you so rightly halted from his vile intent, and it is best to do all that is in one's power to restore her to the path of righteousness. She must certainly be wed, and as soon as possible."

"I am of the same opinion, Father Lawrence. I shall read the banns next Sunday. Tomorrow morning, when I confer with Monsieur Villiers, I shall see to it that he agrees to hold the wedding ceremony not later than two weeks from then. I shall not be able to rest at night until Laurette Boischamp is legally wedded and bedded by this worthy patron, who has made so many charitable contributions to the village and to my own humble church."

"I shall try to reason with the girl," said Father Lawrence. "I have some little experience in these matters, you see."

"Of course, Father Lawrence," Père Mourier said somewhat dolefully. "In one sense it is a pity that this charming maiden cannot be linked to a husband nearer her own age. But who would you have? Our village is humble and poor, and all the vineyards are owned by the patron. The people here are tenant farmers, dependent upon his good charity for their wages and their little cottages. Without his efforts and benign humanitarianism they would be all penniless and out of work, and hence liable to mischievous employment. The devil finds work for idle hands, you know."

"I am acquainted with the proverb," Father Lawrence dryly retorted. "Yes, nature and the call of the senses—which is so often that of the devil himself—urges a liaison of youth to youth. But, domestic bliss with so worthy and affluent a man as you tell me this Monsieur Villiers is, has great virtues to commend it. Especially as he is, as you say, a contributor to the greater glory of Mother Church."

"Exactly my opinion," beamed the obese holy man. "Well, I shall open the door and you shall see this delicious young sinner."

So saying, he turned the knob of the door and the two priests entered. Laurette turned her head and uttered a startled cry of shame and fright, her face turning scarlet to behold a stranger seeing her thus humbled, kneeling on the chair where she had received her scourging.

"Do not be distressed, my daughter," Father Lawrence spoke to her in excellent French. "I am of the same faith as your good father confessor, Père Mourier, and he has told me much about you. I feel already a warm sympathy for you, my daughter."

"Aye, that we both have," seconded the fat French priest.

I need not recount to my readers the tedious and pompous sermon which both men preached to the unhappy, golden-haired Laurette. Suffice it to say that they threatened her with a fall from grace and even excommunication if she did not swear to be chaste and true until the marriage ceremony to her intended husband, and that both strictly forbade her even so much as a whispered conversation with that scoundrel Pierre Larrieu. Father Lawrence ended by warning her that, if she sinned again, Père Mourier would doubtless let her taste the scourge and even more severely than she had already felt it this night. Then Père Mourier volunteered to see Laurette safely back to her parents' abode, and departed from the rectory with her clinging to his arm.

Father Lawrence rubbed his hands gleefully and went back to the salon, where, as he had anticipated, he found the chestnut-haired Amazon awaiting him. "Let me show you to your room, Your Reverence," Desirée invited. Her glowing eyes promised; I could already then have predicted that she meant to share the bed she had prepared in his honor. "It is, alas, only a humble cot. It is not at all worthy of Your Reverence."

"Do not apologize, my daughter," Father Lawrence said smilingly. "It is the spirit and the intention which count. Lead me to this gracious shelter."

She lead him at once to the little room, which was cramped and narrow and, just as she told him, provided only an old cot with a rather worn mattress.

No sooner were they in the room together (out of my Flea-ish curiosity, I had decided to follow them rather than Laurette and Père Mourier), but Father Lawrence inspected the cot by seating himself upon it. "It will bear my weight and that is good enough, my sister," he approved. "We are taught humility and poverty, so I am not one for fine trappings. But tell me now, my daughter, I am told you are a widow like this Madame Bernard. How is it that no one in this village has asked for your hand in marriage, for it seems to me that you are sturdy and comely and well capable of bringing joy to the household of a worthy man."

"The fact is, Your Reverence," the chestnut-haired Amazon chattily retorted with another roguish glance at him, "there is no man in Languecuisse who feels himself endowed enough by nature to satisfy my fleshly longings. And I would not be a burden on any man unless he wished me as his loyal loving consort."

"The attitude that you have is praiseworthy, my daughter. But you may speak freely to me of such things, for I know much about what takes place between husband and wife, having traveled a great deal and observed the foibles of men and the women. Do you mean that the men of this village are frightened off by your tall and magnificent beauty?"

Desirée blushed like a modest virgin at this, and clasped her hands before her and lowered her eyes. "It is not entirely that, Your Reverence. It is true that I am as tall as a man, but I think they are afraid that I will tire them out between the sheets at night. I ask your pardon for speaking so grossly."

"Oh, there is no need to ask for pardon, my child," smiled Father Lawrence. "For heaven looks down with happy gaze upon souls truly united in wedlock who enjoy each other and keep unto themselves once their troth is plighted. But I am still somewhat dense, my dear daughter, as to the precise meaning you imply. Do you mean to tell me there is no man in all this village who can satisfy your physical cravings?"

"None thus far since my poor husband's passing, Your Reverence," Desirée mournfully replied, shaking her beautiful head so her thick chestnut mane danced in the air about her shoulderblades. "And, once again, begging your pardon, even my husband was not sufficient unto me, though of course I knew it would be a sin to seek out the beds of others while I was still his wife."

"Rightly so, my daughter. But now that you are unattached, as it were, you are free to look for such a man. Now tell me, has this good Père Mourier shown any designs upon your person?"

Desirée blushed at this forthright question from a holy man, then giggled at the irreverent thoughts it provoked. "I think he may have, Your Reverence. He saw me this afternoon trampling the grapes in the cask and he stared very boldly at my naked legs and belly. And it was directly after I stepped out of the cask that he proposed that I should become his housekeeper. He asked nothing about my culinary talents, nor any others. But, of course, he has known me for several years as a faithful spouse and one of his parishioners."

"That then explains his interest in you." Father Lawrence had approached the beautiful, tall Amazon. Now he put his hands on her hips and boldly appraised her swelling breasts with knowledgeable eyes. "You seem very young, my daughter."

"Alas, Father, I am twenty-eight. In Languecuisse, this is almost old age for a woman. The young men have eyes only for the damsels like that little Laurette you just met. She is only nineteen, but that too is much older than is customary for marriage in this region."

"All the more reason for her to be wed as soon as possible," Father Lawrence avowed. His hands slipped back now over Desirée's jutting, boldly ripe bottom cheeks, which he squeezed through her thin skirt. "Of a truth, my daughter, you do not feel to be much older than Laurette. And you tell me that there is no man hereabouts whom you deem sufficient to give you physical joy?"

"I said not so far, Your Reverence," Desirée murmured. She stared into his eyes, her red lips curving in a comprehending smile. And she moved closer to him, letting his hands wander as they would. Then she uttered a little gasp and looked down. Between their bodies, there was already a polarity: The cassock of the good father bulged out tremendously from his loins. Furtively, the beautiful chestnut-haired Amazon slipped her hand down and her fingers tentatively closed over the protuberance. "Oh, Your Reverence, I cannot believe it!" she ejaculated in a tremulous voice.

"What cannot you believe, my daughter?" His voice had become hoarse by this time, as might well be imagined. And his fingers grew bolder still, kneading and squeezing the luscious contours of Desirée's bottom through the thin stuff of her skirt.

"That—that you are such a man as heaven should have sent me long ago," the Amazon brazenly murmured, looking deeply into his eyes, her red lips moist and parted with obvious invitation.

"But things are not what they seem at all times, my daughter," he banteringly replied. "Perhaps it would be well to judge by actuality rather than by appearance."

"But I would not dare offend Your Reverence," Desirée murmured apologetically.

"That which is done sincerely is not offensive, my dear child," he smilingly retorted.

At this, the forward young widow stooped, caught up the hem of his cassock and furled the silken garment to his waist, holding it there with one hand while she rummaged rather expertly at his drawers. In a trice she had liberated his sexual weapon, and her eyes widened with amazement at the sight.

Father Lawrence was prodigiously equipped, in full erection at her touch, for Desirée lost no time in clasping the middle of the shaft with her strong fingers to discover the actuality rather than being swayed by the appearance as the good father had put it. But this was surely true: his penis must have measured at least seven and a half inches in length. It was admirably thick as well and the head, which rose out of a narrow groove of circumcision, was oval-shaped and slightly elongated. Its lips were thin and tightly shut together, but they were already twitching with carnal irritation from the bold enclaspment of that beautiful hand.

"I cannot believe my eyes, Your Reverence," she exclaimed, her voice slightly trembling. "I truly would not have believed it!"

"Are you of a mind to test its measure, my

daughter?" he softly inquired.

"Oh, yes, if Your Reverence would so honor a poor humble widow," she breathed.

"Then you had best secure the door sure lest your new master come upon us."

"I will do that at once, Your Reverence. But do not worry about Père Mourier. He and the maiden Laurette will take a long and devious stroll before he reaches her abode, for he wishes to impress upon her the need for chastity. Besides, after he has gone to sleep, I will come to you again and we can have more time—that is, if I do not anger you by my sinfulness."

"But you have committed no sin, my daughter. Yours is a curious inquisitiveness which both delights and inflames me."

She hurried to the door and threw the bolt. Then swiftly she divested herself of her thin skirt and blouse, under which she was as naked as she had been in the cask that afternoon. She stood before him, hands at her sides, head tilted back, blushing deliciously, proud in the knowledge that his eyes roved over her sumptuous breasts, her suave, well-dimpled belly, the thick luxuriant garden of dark chestnut curls which covered her mound and disappeared between her thighs, and those robust yet beautifully proportioned thighs themselves, which appeared capable of crushing a man's ribs within their fiery embrace.

With a gasp of admiration, Father Lawrence drew off his cassock. Taking off his shoes and divesting himself of his drawers, he stood before her equally naked, his body wiry yet vigorous, nowhere showing emaciation or meagerness or age. And least of all did the fulminating structure of his swollen cock evince the least flaccidity of flesh that is so common to men who attain their two score of years and more. Desirée let a sigh of admiration escape her as she moved towards him, her big breasts jiggling with each step. Her nipples were already turgid coral points of erotic anticipation, and voluptuous shivers ran along her thighs and calves at the thought of what awaited her.

She put out one soft hand to cup his heavy, hairy balls, overcharged with amorous essence, and she sighed again. Meanwhile, Father Lawrence, rather than let this judging be one-sided, circled her waist with his left arm and extended his right forefinger toward the thick bush of her pubis, and began to feel for the soft pink lips of Venus themselves. Her slow little giggle and the lascivious squirming of her sumptuous bottom cheeks told him that he had attained his objective. He began to rim the fleshy, soft, and already moistened lips of her cunt with a lingering deliberation which at once told me, expert as I have become in such matters, that he was by no means a novice in the sweet games of Cythera.

Now she used both hands to cup and rub and massage the broad, hot, thickly veined shaft of his organ, and her breasts rose and fell with an erratic tumult as she imagined just how his weapon would feel within her cunt.

"It is so big, so thick and hard and hot, Your Reverence!" she whispered. "Voulez-vous bien me baiser?" (Which, translated, means "Do you really want to fuck me?")

"Once a sword is drawn, it must either draw blood or be sheathed," he quipped. "And since you tell me you are a widow, it follows that you are no virgin, and therefore my blade will not bleed you, my daughter. Let us proceed to sheathe it, then, to your complete satisfaction."

"Oh, yes, Your Reverence," Desirée exclaimed.

Now it was his turn to use both hands as his fingers found the plump, palpitating lips of Desirée's cunt and drew them apart. Meanwhile, the beautiful chestnut-haired Amazon daintily grasped his cock and steered him toward her orifice. The elongated, naked pink tip of his sword forced its way through the thick, curly ringlets which still shielded her secret bower, and then he gave himself a little forward jerk and engaged a good half of his shaft within her channel. Desirée uttered a cry of bliss: "Oh, Your Reverence! It stretches me, it pierces me! Oh, do not stop now, put all of it into me quickly!"

"With the greatest of good will, my daughter," he told her as he took hold of her naked bottom cheeks at the base, sinking his fingers eagerly into that succulent warm flesh, and thrust himself to the very hilt till their hairs mingled. Vigorous and strong though she was, the naked Amazon nonetheless had to clutch him with her arms locked around his shoulders, for she had begun to sway and tremble at the very first dig of his prong in her quivering chasm. She closed her eyes, her nostrils opening and closing furiously as carnal desire swept through her every limb. "Oh, it fills me, it stretches and digs so deliciously," she moaned in her rapture.

His lips found the pulse hollow of her throat as he began to fuck her with long deep thrusts. She let her head fall back, and her fingernails dug into his bare shoulders, excoriating him in her delirium.

"You are very tight, my daughter, yet there is a moistness there which tells me that you are longing for satisfaction," he declared, without once interrupting his slow, deliberate rhythm.

"Oh, it is true, Your Reverence. It has been many a month since I enjoyed so magnificent a cock inside me—oh, it is so good when you push it in slowly. I can feel every inch of it invading and stretching me there!" she gasped.

Now she began to press forward to meet his charger with an undulating twist to her ripe, full hips that showed how furiously she was being drawn towards the zenith of carnal ecstasy. Her nails dug into his flesh almost to the blood, but in retaliation his fingers squeezed and pinched the shuddering cheeks of her succulent backside. Indeed, by tactile means he was able to communicate a kind of signal to her when he meant to thrust home his blade: when he squeezed the edges of both plump cheeks, this was a sign to her that he was delving home to her hairs, whilst when he eased the grip of her behind, that meant she should be ready to expect his withdrawal.

I heard the moist, suctioning sounds which his prong and her well-lubricated channel produced during their in-and-out maneuvering. Desirée's gasps and sighs became louder: "Aaah! Oh, Your Reverence, no one has ever fucked me so well—I entreat you not to stop, it is too heavenly—ooohh, harder, push it in to me till you tear me apart. I am strong and can endure such penance! Eeeeaaaiiiiih!! I cannot hold on much longer, Your Reverence, please, make me spend—now—now! Oh, now!!!"

Sobbing at this final ejaculation, she crushed herself against him so her magnificent naked breasts flattened against his heaving chest. Her teeth nipped at his satiny shoulder as his hands forced open her buttocks and he delved a fingertip into the tight, pink, twitching rosette of her bottomhole. At that very instant, he forced himself forward till his balls clashed against her thick, dark-chestnut pubis, and, with a cry of delight, announced his own fulfillment: "Yes, now, my daughter, take it all!"

I saw her Amazonian body quake and shudder as the tempestuous burst of his essence lashed the volutes of her womb. Their cries coalesced, just as had their flesh, and thus the most ardent widow in all Languecuisse welcomed the virile English ecclesiastic. The widow Bernard would have to be superhumanly endowed to be able to equal, much less surpass, the passionate fervor of this chestnut-haired, bold, flaunting Amazon.

After it was over, Father Lawrence mopped both their private parts with a cambric handkerchief that he then put to his nostrils and inhaled, closing his eyes with rapture at the memento. Desirée swiftly donned her skirt and blouse, then, drawing the bolt, she turned to him, her face radiant, and whispered, "I shall knock three times, Your Reverence, after Père Mourier has begun to snore. Once he does that, I know he will not wake until the dawn."

"Oh?" Father Lawrence chuckled, "so then you have indulged his passions already, my daughter?"

"Oh, no, Your Reverence! But I was told this by his last housekeeper, Dame Clorinda, who left his service some few months ago to wed a rich widower. But I am certain, Your Reverence—and again I beg you to forgive me if my boldness offends you—that even if he does summon me to his bed, he cannot possibly be so competent as you in making me forget my widowhood. I bid you au revoir, Your Reverence."

CHAPTER NINE

The Amazonian widow was right in her earlier observation: Père Mourier did not return to the rectory until a good half-hour after the scene which I have just described. He was in fine spirits and asked Desirée to bring him a little glass of cognac to his bedchamber and invited her to join him with a petite verre for herself.

When she had arrived, he took his glass from the little tray which she had brought and took an appreciative sip, rolling the fiery liquid back and forth in his mouth before swallowing. Then he smacked his belly with a fat hand and buoyantly declared, "That little minx is not nearly so innocent as she pretends."

"Why do you say that, Your Reverence?" the chestnut-haired housekeeper queried.

"Well, she was most meek and deferential, Madame Desirée," the fat priest answered after taking another sip of his cognac. "She promised very dutifully to accept the good Monsieur Villiers as her lawful consort and gave me her word that she would not attempt to communicate with that wretched apprentice of his. The return to her parents' cottage took much longer than I had anticipated, because apparently the poor child had suffered somewhat from the scourging I had given her and hence could not walk too quickly. Indeed, we made several stops along the way to give her respite. I solicitously inquired whether her backside was paining her and she tried most bravely to conceal it from me. Finally, I resorted to seeing for myself and had her truss up her clothes whilst I let down her drawers just to have a look. She was not too badly marked, so I massaged her flesh for her, and that seemed to give her some comfort. But in spite of her blushes and protests that she was dying of shame, the little baggage wriggled her backside about in a way that showed she did not find my caresses too displeasing. Ah, it is fortuitous that she will soon be married and not a temptation any longer for the corrupt and callow young rascals in the community. She is too hot-blooded for her own good. Her husband will know how to assuage her yearnings, I have no doubt."

"That bony old death's-head?" the robust beauty laughingly broke in. "If you want my opinion, Your Reverence, he will not have the strength to make so much as a dent in Laurette's maidenhead."

"Fie upon such impious opinions, with all due respect to yourself, dear Madame Desirée," Père Mourier chided her. "With so lovely a virgin to warm his bed, the patron will surely be roused to good appetite. Why, I am certain that even a stone statue would come to life if it were placed beside that young hoyden!"

"But a man like Your Reverence should know that many men find timid young virgins abhorrent, because they are all tears and false modesty and do not know how to love."

"I will concede that," said the obese holy man, "but marriage is a sacrament not meant solely for the furthering of concupiscence. The joining of the flesh is only incidental to a union of this kind. The good patron wishes to have a bride to cheer his lonely house and to comfort him with her presence, as well as to give him an heir who will one day inherit all his wealth. That will be Laurette's duty, nothing more. As it will be mine to instruct her in her obligations, once she is properly wedded."

"I have no doubt that Your Reverence is a great authority on the matter," Desirée vouchsafed with a sly glow in her dark eyes. "May I bring you another glass of cognac?"

"Not now, my beauty. Your charms are intoxication enough for me at this moment," Père Mourier chuckled. "Did you put our visitor from England to his room and see to his comforts for the night?"

"Oh, yes, Your Reverence. He found the cot quite satisfactory and said that he was in need of a good night's rest after his long journey."

"Good. Then we are alone together, are we not?"

"To the best of my knowledge, Your Reverence."

At this announcement, Père Mourier decided to dispense with meaningless conversation. He rose from his chair and caught the handsome wench about the waist then put his fleshy lips to the jutting tip of one luscious breast as it prodded the thin stuff of her blouse, and bestowed a smacking kiss upon the luscious tidbit. "I must confess to you, Madame Desirée," he panted, "that this afternoon I was smitten by your grace and nimbleness in the cask and that is what made me decide to offer you employment in my humble rectory. I said to myself also that it was a great pity that a strapping young and comely woman like yourself should languish for affection, since you have been bereaved so long without solace."

Desirée giggled and her hands cupped his florid cheeks as she let herself be handled, for now his pudgy fingers had taken possession of her opulent backside and were squeezing the resilient globes through her thin skirt. "Your Reverence is much too kind to a poor widow," she artfully murmured. "Does Your Reverence wish me to accompany him to bed now?"

"You matchless woman, I knew I had made no mistake in employing you for my lonely household," cried the delighted priest as he crushed his lips to hers and drew her tightly against him. His hands kneaded her voluptuous backside, while at the same time his savagely erect weapon jabbed through the silk cassock against her furry crotch, which itself was shielded by a single thickness of cloth. "Yes, yes, this is my dearest wish, Madame Desirée, for, as you can no doubt feel at this very moment, I am longing to fuck you!"

"It would be a great honor for me, Your Reverence, to do my poor best to satisfy your longings. But this is just what I was speaking of a moment ago. Do you not see that a shy maiden like Laurette would be nigh unto swooning if the worthy patron or a far younger and more adequate gentleman like yourself were to make his wants known to her just as you are doing to me now?"

"Your humor enchants me, my beautiful daughter," the fat priest chortled, as he began to kiss her lips and cheeks with moist, smacking testimony of his excited approval. "And I shall try to be worthy of the compliment you have just paid me. Of a truth, I modestly admit that I am somewhat more powerful in amatory conduct than the worthy patron of this little village. So hurry, then, and let us strip to the skin so that I may demonstrate my vigor!"

He released the Amazonian housekeeper and hurriedly drew off his cassock and then his drawers, standing hairy and fat and naked, his enormous cock thrusting out in ferocious impatience. Desirée swiftly divested herself of blouse and skirt then sank down on her knees as if in awe of this fearsome member. "What a mighty cock," she breathed, her eyes wide and glowing in admiration. "It will surely tax me sorely, but I must feel it in my spot. It has been so long since I have known the feeling of a vigorous male shaft cramming into my tight little slit that I am almost fainting with anticipation, Your Reverence! But first I must kiss it to show my master gratitude for his kindness in giving me this post. Do I have Your Reverence's leave?"

"Yes, yes, my daughter, but be quick, because I am so overwrought by the naughtiness of that little vixen Laurette that my powers of self-control are already on the wane," he admonished. Desirée put her fingers to his gnarled, hairy balls and tickled them a moment whilst her full red lips nuzzled the huge plum which was the head of his massively turgid weapon. He uttered a groan of tortured delight at this improvisation. "Hurry, hurry, I am fairly bursting, Madame Desirée," he panted.

"But a moment more, Your Reverence," she purred, looking up at him with a deferential and adoring gaze. "It is so long since I have seen so magnificent a cock that surely you cannot deny me the joy of examining it. Have patience with me, Your Reverence, for this is only my first day as your housekeeper, and it is too soon for me to have learned all your habits."

With this, the wily widow took hold of her magnificent naked breasts and cupped them, pushing them together to create a satiny flesh channel into which she pushed the head of the father's enormous shaft. Pressing her hands firmly against her naked love-globes, she thus imprisoned the holy man's throbbing cock within the velvety, warm cleft, at the same time exclaiming: "Oh, Your Reverence, how hot and hard it is! Do rub yourself back and forth a little so that I may feel its wonders against my bare skin before you put it into me!"

The naked priest was shuddering with sexual fever; he plunged his fingers into the long chestnut tresses of his naked, buxom housekeeper, his face screwed up in torment, and began to comply with her devious request. But he managed to rub only two or three times back and forth between the squeezed-together globes of her bosom before he uttered a hoarse cry and shot forth all his seed. "The devil take it, my daughter, you have made me lose my strength," he whined. The housekeeper promptly rose and scurried to procure a handkerchief from the drawer of his dresser, with which she sponged her sperm-glistening bosom, chest, and throat. Wheedlingly she returned to him, a solicitous look on her boldly lovely features, cooing, "I beg Your Reverence's pardon, for truly I did not mean to offend you. Yet Your Reverence is wonderfully endowed. There will be other times for us, have no fear of that, for it is a great honor and privilege for me to serve Your Reverence in any way I can."

His cock was limp and flaccid now, a sorry sight after its once ferocious state. Père Mourier sighed and shook his head: "Alas, I fear it may be a sign that the moment is not propitious. It is not seemly that I should entertain carnal thoughts upon my housekeeper, for it would appear to you that my association with that forward young minx stimulated me to unnatural desires which I sought to vent upon your defenseless person. I shall go to sleep, my daughter." He uttered another weary sigh as he sank down into bed and promptly closed his eyes.

The naked beauty came to his bedside, bent down and applied a chaste kiss on his forehead, murmuring, "May Your Reverence have sweet dreams, then. I will prepare a delicious breakfast for you and your guest tomorrow."

"My mind is not at this moment on my stomach,"

the fat priest dolefully quipped, "but you have my blessing all the same. A good night to you, Madame Desirée."

"And to you, Your Reverence." The naked beauty made a curtsy. Then swiftly she put back on her blouse and skirt and left the room.

I followed her, as you may well comprehend, back to Father Lawrence's door. It had not been locked, so it was easy enough for the chestnut-haired Amazon to knock three times, then slip inside and bolt it so that no one might interrupt their session. In a moment she had rid herself of blouse and skirt and was Eve-naked. Licking her red lips with the tip of her nimble pink tongue, she rubbed her flanks with nervous hands as she approached the cot on which the English ecclesiastic lay.

"What fair visitation is this?" Father Lawrence murmured as he raised his head.

"It is only myself, Your Reverence. My employer has taken to his bed and will not need me for the rest of the night. Being of a hospitable nature, I wished to look in upon you and see to your comforts," purred the handsome wench. She knelt down beside the cot, leaning towards him so that the opulent fruits of her naked bosom dangled temptingly within reach. He groped out his hand and encountered one of those luscious turrets, his fingers savoring the magnificent love-cantaloupe.

"Your hospitality is the most delicious that has ever been tendered to me, my lovely daughter," he hoarsely murmured. "But I would have you remember that I did not constrain you to make this sacrifice."

"Oh, Your Reverence, it is of my own free will and eagerness. And it is no sacrifice, but rather for my own selfish pleasure. I long to feel your great cock thrusting deep within my little crevice," whispered the beautiful widow. She in turn now stretched out a soft

hand and discovered the rigid, boldly erect structure
of his sexual organ rising between his thighs like a
semaphore. It was this edifice which the charming
wench first touched, as if by unerring instinct. At once
her fingers closed over her prize, not wishing to
relinquish it till it had performed its noble work within
her cunny. "C'est incroyable!" she breathed. "Why, it
is even bigger than the first time. You are surely more
valorous than my worthy employer, who, after but a
single emission of his holy fluid, acknowledged himself
defeated in his desires."

"This is the result of good English beef, daily
constitutionals, long hours of meditation, and a certain
continence in withholding my vigor till a worthy
occasion presents itself," responded the English
ecclesiastic. "But I fear that this cot is far too narrow
to accommodate the two of us for dalliance."

"Oh, begging Your Reverence's pardon, for I
would never dare to contradict so eminent a
personage as yourself. But there is a way, if you will
permit me to show it to you," Desirée murmured
seductively.

"I am always eager to learn new and useful
knowledge, my beautiful daughter," was Father
Lawrence's riposte. At this, the naked Amazon got
astride him. Though it was pitch black in this little
room off the kitchen, her female instincts guided her
towards what she wanted. Crouching over him, she
took hold of his vigorously swollen cock with her left
hand whilst with thumb and median finger of her right
she opened the moist pink lips of her libidinous cunt.
Then, sinking down very slowly, she introduced the
meat of his organ well within the warm lobbyway of
her matrix. "Oh, it is hardly inside me, yet it thrills me
beyond words!" she announced in a breathless
whisper.

Father Lawrence lay prone at his ease, content

to let the chestnut-haired housekeeper take such intimate initiative with him. Desirée sank down a little more, till the head of his throbbing organ moved just into her vaginal sheath. Then, assured that it was well within her keeping, she flattened herself over him, her big juicy breasts mashing hard against his straining chest as his arms welcomed her by clasping together over her smooth satin back. Now in his turn, wanting to imprison her for complete enjoyment, the English priest spread his muscular legs, then clamped them resolutely over the Amazonian widow's rippling, naked thighs. Her hands reached under his shoulders to grip him tenaciously as she groaned with pleasure to feel his massive organ dig to the very roots within her churning love-canal.

"Ahh, how good it is," she moaned. "You pack me so tightly that my poor little spot can hardly breathe! Oh, let us lie like this a long while, so that I can summon all my poor strength to deal with such a monster inside of me!"

"I will give it to your keeping with full confidence and trust, my daughter," he panted. Retaining his left arm around her sculptured naked back, Father Lawrence groped along her spinal column till he had reached the shadowy, narrow cleft between her jouncy bottom cheeks. Desirée, comprehending his motive, wriggled and squirmed till his fingertip brushed the sensitive rosebud of her behind. Having attained his objective, he pried the tiny hole apart and inserted his finger to the knuckle then began to move it about slowly in her nether passageway.

"Aaahh, I shall die of pleasure from it, Your Reverence!" the beautiful naked widow sobbed. She fused her mouth to his and swirled her pink tongue against his own. Her nipples were daggers of flinty-hard passion as they scraped against his heaving chest, and her body was aglow with erotic energy. Now slowly she lifted her hips a little, feeling his ramrod grudgingly recede from the innermost crannies of her hot, voracious cunt. Her groan of delirium was matched by his own gasp of rapture; his forefinger dug to the very hilt within her bottomhole. Thus stimulated, the naked housekeeper sank down and impaled herself to the very hairs. Now his tongue was the aggressor and thrust between her parted lips to fan the flames of her furious lasciviousness. The cot creaked its protest against their combined weight, but they paid it no heed.

"What a great pity, Your Reverence," Desirée gasped, "that Père Mourier engaged me just before you arrived in Languecuisse! Oh, how good it is to feel you in both my crevices—oh, I beg of you, do not stop what you are doing to me, it is divine! With all respect to his holiness, I should have loved being your housekeeper instead—aahhh, you are bringing me close, Your Reverence!"

"Never mind, my eager daughter," Father Lawrence gasped as he renewed his zeal, arching now to meet her wriggling perorations on his manly harpoon, all the while plunging his finger in and out of her quaking nether chasm, "during my sojourn in this charming village, I shall be happy to act as your confessor at any time you choose—always understanding, of course, that my worthy colleague and brother in the faith does not otherwise occupy you at the times you choose to visit me. Now, my daughter, the moment is at hand for me as well. Let me feel your responding strength!"

As he dug his finger to the hilt a final time and arched himself so that his furiously burdened cock could probe to the deepest recesses of her Venus, Desirée uttered a shrill shriek of ecstasy, which the good father promptly smothered by covering her mouth with his. Their bodies writhed and quaked in savage chaos, till at length they rolled off the cot onto the floor where they expired simultaneously amid sobbing and groaning gasps of mingled rapture.

Perching on the edge of the sagging cot, I watched with growing admiration as Father Lawrence, finding himself now in command of the situation—by rolling off, he had managed to come atop and astride his beautiful mount—at once began to fuck her again with an even greater voracity.

"Ohhh, Your Reverence," Desirée breathed, "what a marvel you are! Even though I still feel your hot spunk seething in my vitals, your blade is still wonderfully hard—oh, how it digs inside of me and finds tiny niches which it had not touched before—oh, why did not Providence grant that you saw me first?"

"It is not mete to question the will of Providence, my daughter," Father Lawrence gently admonished her without losing a single beat in his vigorous rhythm of plowing her well-lubricated cleft. "Is it not enough for you that I am employing your excellent services now? This is the trouble with the world: it pines for fantasies and does not show gratitude for what it is granted. Always remember that, my child. Now hold me tightly in your beautiful arms, and clasp your firm thighs over my buttocks so that I may not become unsaddled as we ride towards our Elysian bliss together!"

Desirée at once complied and locked him with her magnificent, sturdy, satiny thighs, while he accelerated his thrusts till her face turned this way and that as a second transport neared. Once again she opened her mouth to cry out her fervent thanks for the excitement he had evoked within her loins, but the good father silenced her as he had done before. His lips and tongue feasted on hers, and they rolled over and over on the floor as the paroxysm struck them both at the same time.

When at last tranquillity had calmed their inflamed senses, it was the Amazonian housekeeper who first cried a halt to this tryst, saying that she would fain spend the rest of the night in the arms of so demanding an employer, but must humbly beg a respite so that she might get up early at dawn to prepare Père Mourier's breakfast.

When she finally crept out of the little room, she went back to hers with the lagging step of one who is joyously fatigued. Her soft sighs were like wafting summer breezes, a sign that, for the time at least, the insatiable passions of this magnificent Amazon were satiated. As for Father Lawrence, he went back to his cot, stretched himself out on his back, pillowing his head on his arms, and fell fast asleep with a smile on his face that was doubtless an expression of the pleasure he took in so warm a welcome to this little village in Provence.

CHAPTER TEN

The next day was virtually a holiday because the celebration of the harvest had caused the villagers to drink copiously of the good wine and many quaffed in excess and then slept like the dead till nearly noon. Besides, there was, I am quite sure, a veritable orgy of fornication in every cottage, and this physical excess coupled with over-indulgence in wine brings a delicious torpor even to the young and vigorous. At any rate, Père Mourier, after having his breakfast, left the rectory about noon to pay another call on Monsieur Claude Villiers for the purpose of making certain that the banns between that estimable patron and the virgin Laurette would officially be read the following Sunday. Also, as he informed Desirée, he wished to visit Laurette and her parents after having seen the patron so that there would be clarification on the part of all concerned in this important ceremony. Father Lawrence, who woke a little before the obese French priest, shared breakfast with him, and apologetically requested that he, rather than Père Mourier, be allowed to speak on his own behalf to Madame Hortense Bernard with the aim of securing board and shelter during his stay in Languecuisse.

"I would not wish to inflict myself sight unseen on the worthy widow, dear colleague," he told the French priest. "You see, if you were to speak to her, she would naturally accept me in advance without ever having laid eyes on me, simply because you have her full confidence. And since I am here in Languecuisse on holiday, and not in my official ecclesiastical capacity, I wish to be sure that she does not find me displeasing as a lodger."

"Such delicacy and tact is admirable, my illustrious confrère," Père Mourier beamed. "I fear the visits to M'sieu Villiers and Laurette will consume much time, since they too require diplomacy and deference. And I know you are eager to settle down to your well-earned comforts whereas, alas, we are too small and crowded to tender you the hospitality you deserve. By all means, call upon the good Widow Bernard, and mention my name. It will suffice, I am certain."

"Believe me, Père Mourier, I have nothing but the highest praise for the gracious hospitality I have been accorded here. Indeed, were I to leave your pleasant little hamlet this very day and never return, I should carry with me the warmest memories of that hospitality."

Father Lawrence then glanced slyly up at the Amazonian housekeeper, who was at that moment, pouring out another cup of coffee for her obese employer. Her face flamed and she very nearly dropped the pewter pot. That she caught it was fortunate indeed for Père Mourier, as the liquid was scalding hot. Had it splashed into his lap, it might well have burned his cock and unmanned him.

"Well, well, that is kindly said," Père Mourier beamed. "But I trust that since you will be quartered not far from my humble rectory, you will not be a stranger once you have established yourself in the abode of Madame Bernard. And now I must be off to spread the good word and to put Laurette, that mischievous little vixen, and our saintly upholder of Languecuisse, into a rapport that will lead them up to the altar."

He left the room, and Desirée at once sidled up to Father Lawrence, her bold eyes warm with remembered felicity from their night together. "Your Reverence will leave me desolate," she murmured seductively. "How shall I endure your absence for an entire month, knowing all the while that you are exposed to the temptation of the impudent trollop Hortense Bernard?"

"But, my daughter," he cried, feigning alarm at this piece of news, "do you imply that I am to be lodged with a sinful woman?"

"Just so, Your Reverence. It is well known that her husband took to drink as a result of her infidelities and also because he could not keep up with servicing her insatiable and lewd demands. Yes, it is true! On the night that he was drowned in the wine vat, he had been turned out of his own cottage by that shameless hussy so that she might entertain a handsome tinker who was passing through that day. He had gone to console his sorrows in the arms of Jacqueline Aleroute, the plump wanton who is wife to the old baker, Henri. And he was just easing himself into her welcoming arms when, as luck would have it, Henri came home earlier than was his wont, for it was his custom to stop at the tavern after he baked his bread for the next day and to finish a bottle of Chablis. Surprised in the very act of cuckolding the old baker, poor Gervaise—that was the name of Hortense's husband, Your Reverence—clambered out of the window. But, as his trousers were dangling about his legs, he stumbled and fell into the wine vat."

"That story is a tragic one, my daughter. But perhaps my presence in the abode of Madame Bernard will serve as an ameliorative influence. Through my counsel and guidance, she may be able to wrest the demon of carnal temptation from her spirit."

"Perhaps, Your Reverence," Desirée said,

shaking her handsome head. "But I fear she will seek to lure you to her shameless bed. The mere sight of a man sets her lusts aflame. And worst of all—oh, but I blush to relate it before Your Reverence!"

"Speak freely and frankly, my daughter, for there is no mortal sin with which I am not familiar. The more one knows of the devil's subtle ways of corruption, the better one is armed against them."

"Yes, that is true, Your Reverence. Well—oh, but truly, it is so shameful that I blush even to hint of it!"

He fitted his arm round her little waist and gazed up at her with a benevolent smile as he gently responded, "I pardon you in advance, and compliment you on your modesty, my daughter. Now tell me honestly what penchant of Madame Bernard's so horrifies you."

Desirée shivered as his arm tightened round her waist. Quickly, she bent to his ear and whispered, her opulent bosom rising and falling quickly in her emotions.

"You are certain that she prefers to be buggered, my daughter?"

"Shh, Your Reverence, you must not say such wicked words!" gasped the Amazonian housekeeper, her face crimson with sensual titillation.

"There is nothing wicked in words, my child, only in deeds. Well, then, be of good cheer, for I promise you I shall reason and remonstrate with this unfortunate woman, who has not enjoyed your ascent to grace by being engaged as the housekeeper of a goodly man of the Church. I shall leave now to make the acquaintance of this misguided creature, my child. Count your blessings to yourself after I am gone."

"Yes, surely." Desirée let a languorous sigh escape her. "Alas, Your Reverence!"

"What troubles you?" He rose and drew her to

him, his hands squeezing the firm, jutting globes of her sumptuous backside through her skirt. "You need keep no secrets from me, my daughter, as I think you know already."

"I-I shall be l-lonely without Your Reverence here to console me," Desirée whimpered, her face downcast.

"Courage, my beautiful daughter! Tilt up that lovely face and give me a parting kiss of peace. I promise that you shall not be forgotten in my prayers, nor my thoughts either. If ever you are stricken with despair or aught else that troubles you greatly which your worthy employer cannot alleviate for you, I give you leave to call upon me at Madame Bernard's abode." So saying, the English ecclesiastic cupped her trembling chin with one hand and fused his lips to hers, while she wriggled lasciviously against him. Her tongue crept out and furled into his mouth as her arms wrapped around him, loath to release him. "Ohh, please, Your R-Reverence," she breathed tremulously, "will you not appease my loneliness a last time before you depart? I am sure that once you go to reside with that lewd trollop, Hortense Bernard, you will be so preoccupied trying to cast the demon out of her that you will have no time for your humble servant, Desirée."

"You must learn patience and discipline, my child," he murmured. "There is not time for me to allay your grief completely, but I will grant you a momentary respite for your sufferings. Hoist your skirt and petticoat and keep them at your waist, while you continue kissing me farewell."

"I-I have no petticoat on, Y-Your Reverence," Desirée quavered.

"So much the better, then less time will be lost," he retorted.

The Amazon swiftly tucked up her skirt, under

which she was voluptuously naked, and kept it wadded up in a roll above her belly with one trembling hand, while her other foraged at once to his cassock just at the point where his sexual weapon flourished. But the English ecclesiastic halted her and shook his head. "No, my daughter," he said kindly but firmly. "You must learn the lesson of forbearance. I alone will ease your anguish, but you must withhold yourself in all other ways. Use that soft hand to clamp against my back to support you, and now give me your soft red lips."

She reluctantly obeyed. Once his lips crushed against hers, he clamped his left arm around her pliant waist and approached his right forefinger to the thick, dark, chestnut bush which hid her pink-lipped cunny. Delicately, he began to frig the beautiful Amazon, the tip of his wiry finger just grazing the quivering, coral petals of her cunt hole, till the voluptuous young widow began to gasp and sigh and to squirm herself this way and that. "Do not let your skirt fall, my daughter, or I shall stop at once," he warningly teased her, "and continue to kiss me lovingly to signify your sorrow in our parting."

Her burning lips fervently mashed to his, and her tongue voraciously dug between his lips, scraping his teeth and gums, while her fingers, like talons, clawed at his sinewy back. His forefinger resumed its caresses over the labia of her Venus, which at once grew moist and began to twitch and grow a darker pink, inflamed from the lustful desires which his titillations evoked. Her eyes dilated enormously and then became misty with her swiftly rising passions as she breathed, "Ohh—ahhhh—ohhh, ahh, Y-Your R-Reverence—oh, I implore you not to torture me like this, but to plough my furrow with that hard rod of yours. It is what I so dearly need, if I am to be denied it for the future!"

"Think upon the communion I granted you last

night, my daughter, for its exemplary vigor should not be so soon forgotten," was his bantering response, "and remember this invaluable precept: Anticipation is sometimes even more rewarding than realization. Better still, summon your inventive mind to pretend that what you feel between your sturdy thighs is that which you enjoyed last night to such overweening measure, since what I now deign to accord you is also a member and part of me."

"Aii—ohh—ahh—y—yes—Y-Your Reverence," moaned the passionate Amazon, whose loins had begun to writhe and jerk convulsively as his clever frigging drove her towards gushing climax, "but the other m-member was ever so much longer and thicker—ahhh!"

"Ingratitude is the curse of the world, my daughter," he said sententiously as he kept frigging her pouting cunt lips, while now his left hand gripped the scruff of her neck to force her to kiss him without ceasing. "That I attend your needs at all when I have errands to perform this day must show you that I hold you in some esteem, so be content. Am I not quieting your fervor somewhat?"

"Ahh—oouuuu—ahrrr—y-yes—ohh, Y-Your R-Reverence," Desirée fairly sobbed, "but it takes so long with your finger—ohh, if only your great rod were stuffed inside me to the very roots, my fondest memories of Your Reverence would be magnified a thousand-fold—ahrrr—ohh, quickly, in mercy, for I am burning up inside my slit!"

"Kiss me gratefully then, my child, and I will see to your assuagement," he whispered. When again her feverish, hot and moist lips crushed on his and once more her nimble tongue flicked and serpentined between his lips, Father Lawrence deftly sought with his questing fingertip the little nodule of her clitoris, sweetly hidden in its fold of soft pink love-flesh, wherein was contained all the potency of her sexual fever. No sooner had he grazed this simulation of a male cock than it throbbed and stiffened, and a moaning, inchoate cry escaped the writhing housekeeper. Her thighs shook with tremors, and she was hard put to retain her uptrussed skirt against her belly, but his left hand supported her by tightening its grip against her neck.

Tantalizingly, he rubbed the little button of her erotic grotto till she was beside herself and the most uncontrollable spasms shook her as she pressed and arched against him, employing all her wiles—even those of her fiercely cajoling tongue that sloshed about so avidly on his mouth—to seduce him into fucking her. But with heroic self-control Father Lawrence resisted her temptation (for a reason that will soon be made manifest to my readers), simply contenting himself with prodding her clitoris this way and that till at last Desirée announced her flooding climax with a raucous cry of rapture and flung both arms 'round his neck while her body jerked and writhed its frenzied responses. He wiped off his copiously bedewed forefinger on her rumpled skirt, then kissed her chastely on the forehead and told her he would remember her in his meditations. And then, while she retired, weeping disconsolately, to the kitchen to see to Père Mourier's afternoon nourishment, Father Lawrence left the rectory.

The cottage of the widow whom the good Père Mourier had recommended as a possible housekeeper was not far from the rectory, a pleasant stroll through verdant fields and hedges, not unlike that which Laurette Boischamp had taken the night before. Father Lawrence walked slowly, enjoying the landscape, the blue sky, and warm sun, serenely at his ease. At length he came to the little cottage and rapped upon the door for admittance, whereupon it was opened by a stunningly buxom female, the sight of whom at once brightened the worthy ecclesiastic's eye.

"Oh, mon père," the woman exclaimed, putting a hand to her mouth, "has something happened to Père Mourier that you are here to replace him?"

"Be of good cheer, my daughter," Father Lawrence at once responded in quite passable French, "your concern for my confrère tells me in what high esteem you hold him. He, on the other hand, spoke warmly to me only last night, praising your zeal and devotion as one of his parishioners."

"The dear man," the widow cooed, raising her eyes to heaven, "may he be forever blessed! But then is it that Languecuisse is to have two priests, Your Reverence?"

"No, Madame Bernard, I am just here on my holiday before I return to the seminary in England where I shall take up my duties," he smilingly informed her. "But, as I am a stranger here, Père Mourier was good enough to suggest that you might be willing to give me board and lodging, for which I will pay you well. I seek privacy and quiet for my meditations, and I would not intrude upon you in the slightest."

During this little speech, the buxom female openly eyed the virile, mature English churchman, while he more discreetly surveyed her charms, recalling what Desirée had mentioned of her carnal foibles. Hortense Bernard was not much older than Desirée—perhaps two or three years at the most—with light brown hair that fell in a lustrous sheaf to her shoulders. She was blessed with a winsome, round face, widely spaced large, soft, brown eyes, a Grecian nose whose broadly flaring wings indicated a sensual temperament, as did the small but overripe lips of her red mouth.

But it was her figure which demanded the most

attention. Even the wide skirt which she wore could not disguise the truly juicy curves of full, appetizing haunches, of robust and sturdy thighs well able to bear many a vigorous charge from the spunk-laden weapon of a lusting male. The fine, plump, well-turned calves were bare, and their skin was of a fine carnation tinting that would whet the sexual appetites of even such a discriminating philosopher of womankind's foibles as Father Lawrence had already proved to be. As to her bosom, the low-cut blouse accentuated its sumptuous treasures: two narrowly set, high-perched round melons boasted wide, pale coral circles from which rose darling pink-hued tidbits that fairly made Father Lawrence's mouth water, if I am any judge of the look in a man's eyes when he gazes upon a female.

I rested on his left shoulder, conserving my powers, for I too was on holiday. The warm sun, the languorous climate, had made me pleasantly drowsy ever since my arrival. I also spent considerable time admiring the widow's charms. Don't get me wrong, my interest was not as would be a man for a woman, nor was it the interest of an insect for a meal—as for sustenance, I had already dined enough soon after coming to Languecuisse to be able to quell the occasional bloodsucking urge which rose in me from time to time. What interested me most, dear reader, was the unfolding of this rather complex relationship between the fat French priest, the tender Laurette and her ill-starred lover, Pierre, the Amazonian Desirée, and Father Lawrence. Somehow, I believed, that before the last-named's stay in this village should come to an end, there would be amusing and dramatic episodes to include in my memoirs and remember fondly in my old age. For even a Flea can gradually lose his powers, very much like a man, and thereby be relegated to recounting his primal urges with fond, burning reminiscences.

"Oh, Your Reverence, it would be a great honor for me to give you shelter in my humble cottage," the Widow Bernard remarked, with a great fluttering of long, thick, curly eyelashes and a charming blush that would have done credit to a girl in her tenderest years. "Since my poor husband died, I have had an empty room, which saddens my heart each time I pass it, for it was in that very chamber that my loving Gervaise and I came together in connubial joy." She sniffled fetchingly and modestly lowered her eyes. I could see that Father Lawrence was already smitten and well on his way to forgetting his recent clandestine delights with Desirée. He was near quivering with eagerness to have Widow Bernard to himself.

"It is most generous of you, my daughter, and heaven will bless your thoughtfulness," he told her with an unctuous smile. "Here is ten francs for the first week of my lodging. I trust there will be sufficient left to purchase such little food as I may require."

"Oh, Your Reverence, with so much money I can easily feed you on roast goose and tender duckling," exclaimed the delighted widow. "Do honor me by entering my humble abode and letting me show Your Reverence to his room. No man has entered it since poor Gervaise left this world on the journey to his eternal reward, which I daily pray he has attained by now."

"Amen to that," said Father Lawrence. "Do go ahead of me, Madame Bernard, to show me the way."

The buxom widow inclined her head deferentially and went forward whilst he followed her. His eyes fixed on the swing of her magnificent spacious hips, watching the undulations of her truly remarkable backside, which her thin skirt clung to and clearly showed with each step. I remembered what Desirée had intimated about the Widow Bernard's predilection, and I was sure the virile English churchman had the same thought in his mind. I myself could attest to her being superbly endowed to service the unnatural lust of a man who was interested in that particular perversity that was often associated with the infamous city of Sodom.

She opened a narrow door and again inclined her head as he entered. The furnishings comprised a low bedstead, a chest of drawers, a footstool and a sturdy, short-backed chair. There was a tiny window placed at about the height of a man's shoulders. Father Lawrence went to it and stared out with a satisfied smile on his lips. "A really exquisite chamber, Madame Bernard. There is all the privacy I could wish for. I am grateful to you."

"But it is I who am beholden to you, Your Reverence. Ten francs—oh, it is a bounty from heaven itself!" She gushed and seizing his hand, bore it to her lips and kissed it.

Benignly, he patted her head with his other hand and responded, "You do me too much credit, my daughter. What is money but something to be shared? And now, with your permission, I will enjoy a little nap, that I may regain my strength."

"Certainly, Your Reverence, certainly," the buxom widow cooed, her voice low and sweet and fawningly deferential as she backed out of the room and then closed the door.

Father Lawrence unpacked his valise and found room for his few articles of clothing. Then, removing his cassock and his little cornered hat and placing them atop the chest, he stretched out on the bed clad only in his drawers since the weather was still extremely warm. Yet no sooner had he closed his eyes and emitted a sigh of content than I perceived a gradual swelling at the crotch of his drawers. Before very long his virile cock was in gigantic erection. Perhaps he was dreaming of his tryst with Desirée, or perhaps of an imagined tryst with virginal Laurette, I cannot tell; but whatever the cause, his organ was readied to decimate a hundred maidenheads.

About ten minutes later there was a discreet tap at the door but Father Lawrence made no sign of having heard it; his breathing was regular, his eyes were closed, and his massive organ stood up like a totem pole. Presently, the door opened very slightly, and the Widow Bernard peeped inside. Not hearing a sound from her new lodger, she opened it a little more and stepped inside the room. At once she beheld the mighty protuberance and her brown eyes widened whilst a delicious rosy color suffused her cheeks. She approached the bed on tiptoe and bent down to stare at this symbol of virility, her lips forming an O of astonishment. At that very moment, Father Lawrence opened his eyes and regarded her.

"Is something amiss, Madame Bernard?" he asked.

Her blushes spread as she hastily turned her gaze from his loins to his chest, and she stammered, "Oh—n-no, Y-Your Reverence, I-I merely came in to ask whether you might not wish something to eat when you waken. Not knowing that you were to board with me, I have very little in my larder. Since I have to go to market, I wished to ask you what your preference was."

"I shall eat whatever you eat, Madame Bernard. Do not go to any trouble on my account, I pray you."

"A-as Y-Your Reverence wishes," Madame Bernard stammered. But she made no attempt to withdraw, and once again, as if by hypnosis, her eyes again riveted upon that upraised structure, which looked about to burst out of the priest's drawers.

He returned her gaze levelly. "Did you wish to tell me anything else, Madame?" he politely inquired.

"N-no, Y-Your Reverence," she quavered. Her

fists were clenched at her sides, and her sumptuous bosom seemed to rise and fall with an erratic rhythm. The fiery hue of her blushes had spread to her throat and dainty little ears.

Wishing to draw her from this curious state of fixation which rendered her incapable of moving from the spot, Father Lawrence gave her a long, meaningful look and then said in a calm tone, "You stare at my cock, Madame Bernard, as if it were a unique phenomenon. I do not seek to offend your gentle modesty, but I deem it necessary to explain that this condition is natural to me when I am completely at my ease. I would not have you think that it is meant by way of assault upon your undisputed virtue."

"Ohh, Y-Your Reverence. I-I did not th-think that at all," the blushing widow gasped, "for certainly a man of Your Reverence's quality would never deign to take notice of so lowly a person as myself. But—but your c-cock is so s-swollen that I could not help looking at it."

"You must not disparage yourself, my daughter," was his mellow reply. "Your kindness in granting me shelter during my sojourn in Languecuisse at once elevates you above many in this charming village. Besides which, you are handsome and comely of face and body, and I marvel that no righteous man has taken the place of your late husband."

Hortense Bernard lowered her eyes and faintly admitted, "I-I have tried to find a man who would take the place of my poor Gervaise, but there are few who can compare with him, Your Reverence. Of—of course, he had his weaknesses too...."

"As do we all, my daughter."

"Yes, Your Reverence. I was going to say, my poor Gervaise did not always come to bed with me as often as I would have wished, though he was very much a man like Your Reverence. I-I mean...."

She turned aside, woefully embarrassed to have been so bold, but Father Lawrence, far from being wroth over her bawdiness, encouraged it by pursuing: "You do not offend me, my daughter, in likening me to a worthy consort who gave you pleasure, and it is pleasing when man and wife take satisfaction, for true marriages are made in heaven."

"I-I am sure of that, Your Reverence. It was only that Gervaise—well, he did not take his joy when it was offered, and, well, we often quarreled over that. Looking back now, I repent my sinfulness, Your Reverence. I-I asked him to—to do things to me that he swore were not proper even between husband and wife. And so he took to drink and forsook my bed."

"Nothing that is done in love between man and woman can be improper, my daughter. It is a pity he did not comprehend this great maxim."

"Oh, yes," she sighed, twisting her fingers nervously about and still averting her scarlet face from his gaze.

"Perhaps it will ease your troubled heart to reveal to me the nature of the dissension between you and your deceased spouse, Madame Bernard," he prompted.

"Ohh, Y—Your Reverence, I should never dare!" she breathed.

"But unless I know I can hardly prescribe for your distress, my daughter. Come, I have told you I am on holiday from my order for this entire month, so regard me rather as a sympathetic friend and not a Grand Inquisitor," he affably remonstrated.

"You—you will not sc-scold me?" she whispered.

"Not one whit, I promise. Quickly, speak!" he urged, sitting up on the edge of the bed and taking her trembling hand.

She hung her head like a little girl caught in mischief and finally blurted out, in a very tremulous voice, "I-I sometimes wished Gervaise to—to take me from—from behind, in the way I-I have seen animals couple in the field."

"Why, that is but following the example set by nature. How, then, could he take offense?"

The buxom young widow squirmed and turned her face aside while she furtively tried to draw her hand away from his, but Father Lawrence held on tenaciously, persisting: "Be honest with me, my daughter. Once you have disclosed the secrets you have hidden in your mind because they trouble you, they will no longer be a source of distress to you."

"Y-yes, Y-Your Reverence," Hortense Bernard stammered, more and more embarrassed. "It—it wasn't only taking me from behind that—that my husband objected you, you see."

"But I do not see at all, my daughter. Be more explicit!"

"Oh, d-dear! It—it is so difficult for me to speak of such delicate things to—to a man of the cloth, Your Reverence."

"But that is precisely why it will be helpful to you to reveal your problems, my daughter, since men of my ilk are more worldly and comprehend better the complex difficulties which beset the uninformed. Speak, I pray you!"

"I-I wished him to put his c-cock into the other place, Your Reverence."

"The other place?" Father Lawrence again feigned ignorance. "Why do you not show me, for actual illustration is always enlightening. Take off your skirt, and indicate to me this other place to which you allude."

By this time, his cock had attained its full girth and length and was even more formidably rigid before her dilated, humid eyes. Hortense Bernard drew a long quivering breath, and then, eyes downcast, tremblingly unhooked her skirt and let it fall about her trim ankles. It was at once apparent that she wore nothing under the skirt, for the soft curves of her carnation-skinned belly appeared, marked by a wide and shallow navel-niche, and below that a thicket of light brown curls which flourished most luxuriantly over the plump aperture of her cunt. Before he could exclaim upon this revelation, she had turned her back and put a quivering forefinger towards the narrow, shadowy groove which separated two magnificently ripe, upstanding round hemispheres. "It—it was in here, Y-Your Reverence," she whispered. "I wished Gervaise to put his th-thing here. But he said it was wickedness to do so. I begged him to do so as a mark of his husbandly affection, for I was always willing, nay, eager, for him to possess me the regular way. Yet he rebuked me."

The English ecclesiastic's eyes blazed at the sight of those bewitchingly jutting bottom globes and promptly extended a hand to stroke and caress their velvety rotundities. Hortense Bernard started and looked 'round with widened eyes at his gentle caress; in an excess of false modesty, she clapped her other hand over her furry slit. "He was wrong to deny you what you sought, my daughter," he at last pronounced in a voice that was hoarse and unsteady, "particularly since you did not shirk your expected marital duties. You sought only a special mark of affection, yet he pitilessly denied you."

"Yes, that is true, Your Reverence," the beautiful half-naked widow sniffed.

"Do you still harbor these desires, my child? Do you still long to be buggered?"

Hortense Bernard closed her eyes, and a long voluptuous shiver rippled down her back as she faintly avowed, "Y-yes, Your R-Reverence."

"Then I will offer myself to accommodate your

needs, my child. Unless my offer offends you?"

"Oh, no!" the brown-haired widow breathed, glancing down again at his mighty cock. The tip of her pink tongue delicately circled the corners of her quivering lips hinting at the excitement she felt at this unforeseen boon.

"Then I must prepare the terrain first. Lie across my lap, my daughter," he instructed. As soon as she had blushingly complied, he circled her waist with his left arm, raised his right hand and dealt her a slap on the ripe summit of one of her velvety naked bottom cheeks, which left the bright pink outline of his chastening palm.

"Ohh!" she gasped, glancing fearfully back, doubtless wondering how this interlude was to lead her to the Sodomic bliss she so yearned for.

"Do not move, my daughter," he bade her, applying a lusty second slap on the other nether globe, which left an even brighter mark on her fair soft skin. "A little spanking will warm your backside and arouse your blood and muscular tone, thereby preparing you for what would otherwise by a somewhat trying ordeal."

Reassured that the Father had not changed his mind and decided to punish her for her wicked desire, Hortense Bernard closed her eyes and clenched her fists, submitting herself to this "preparation." Her naked loins wriggled lasciviously over Father Lawrence's frenziedly bulging crotch, no doubt taxing his own Herculean powers of self-control to the very utmost, but manfully he continued despite this tantalizing distraction to apply vigorous slaps all over the twin hemispheres of her succulent rump till it was scarlet and she was sobbing and wriggling and kicking in the most exciting way.

"Now I think we may proceed to the gratification of your secret desires, my daughter," he remarked in a thick voice that shook with lust. "Remove your blouse and get on the bed on all fours, your legs well spread apart to ease the penetration."

Slowly the young widow clambered up from his lap and after first rubbing her flaming bare bottom energetically, divested herself of her blouse. Getting onto the bed, naked as the day of her birth, head bowed, palms bearing down on the counterpane, knees widely straddled, she presented him with the mouth-watering spectacle of her furiously inflamed backside. By contrast, her untouched thighs and calves gleamed with a soft sheen that was exquisite to behold.

He rose, too, and removed his drawers, giving his massive cock free rein. For a lingering moment he squeezed and massaged her scarlet buttocks with appraising fingers, while the beautiful naked widow whimpered and wriggled till at last he pried open those Calliphygian hillocks and exposed the crinkly little rosebud of her arsehole. The dainty lips contracted with becoming modesty, which only served to inflame Father Lawrence the more, judging by the throbbing movements of his swollen cock. Keeping the globes opened with thumb and median finger of his left hand, he approached his right forefinger to the loft rosette and caressed it a bit, while his willing victim moaned and sighed incoherently, then gently intruded just the tip of his finger within the narrow lobbyway of that furtive little cleft dedicated to the perversities of Sodom.

"Ohh, Your Reverence!" she breathed, her hips jerking fitfully with this preliminary probing.

"Patience, my daughter," he admonished. "I have the wherewithal to satisfy your longings, and I ask only your unmitigated cooperation to produce the result you have so long petitioned for."

He withdrew his finger, moistened it with a

copious amount of saliva, and then anointed the crinkly cleft, again causing her to shift on her knees and to weave her hips in the most lubricious manner. Next, spitting on his right forefinger and median finger a second time, he rubbed the moisture over the fulminating head of his surgingly rigid cock and thence over the tautly drawn, heavily-veined shaft. "Now we shall essay a matching of measurements, my daughter," he told her. "Do not retreat when you first feel me make inroads into that tight chamber or the good work will have to be repeated."

"Oh, no—no, Y-Your Reverence," she moaned, shuddering with erotic fervor.

He put both hands to work against the quaking summits of her inflamed backside, opening them voluminously till the dainty niche itself was lewdly distended and gaped in readiness for his adventuring. He fitted the nozzle of his organ to the orifice, edging it forward with two or three tentative pushes, till at last the muscle grudgingly gave way to his superior strength and accepted just the tip of his formidable cockrod. A low groan of bliss escaped the naked patient, who bowed her head still lower and dug her fingers into the counterpane to steel herself against the assault.

"Now to the good work," he gasped, and thrust vigorously. Hortense, grinding her teeth, met the charge with heroic resistance as his cock slowly dug forward into the narrow channel. From what Desirée had told him, she was certainly not virgin in that crevice, but she remained virtually as tight as a virgin, a circumstance which magnificently implemented Father Lawrence's carnal joy in servicing her thus. By now, a solid inch of his rigid weapon was engulfed in that warm, narrow cavern and visible contractions made her bottom cheeks quake and shudder against his compressing hands.

"Brace yourself again, my daughter. I return to the task," he panted, and with a jerk of his loins sent his cock delving deeper still; a muffled cry escaped from her panting lips as nearly half of the English ecclesiastic's turgid lance burrowed inside her rectal canal.

He halted himself, shuddering to feel the rudely distended passageway spasmodically clutch against his embedded organ in a series of convulsive pressures that compelled him once again to exert the utmost self-discipline in not yet releasing the gouts of spunk.

"Am I hurting you, my daughter?" he solicitously demanded, his voice trembling and hoarse with the ferocious lubricity now rampant within him.

"Ohh, Y-Your Reverence," Hortense Bernard panted, "it is all that I can bear—no man before has ever stretched me so fairly—aaaahh, oh, give me a moment to regain my strength so that I may enjoy all of you within me!"

"Right willingly, my child," he breathed, "for I, too, am in need of respite. But do you bow your forehead to the counterpane; thereby you will angle up your backside all the more delightfully for my thrusting."

The comely young widow willingly complied while her thighs began to quake and threatened to give way beneath her. She was near-fainting with ecstasy. Father Lawrence crouched forward and extended his left hand under her to cup one of her ripe breasts, which he squeezed lovingly. At the same time he groped his right forefinger towards the little lodestone of her clitoris. When he had attained the latter objective, Hortense Bernard uttered a sobbing cry of indescribable delight: "Aiiii, ohhhh, you will make me die with pleasure, Your Reverence! I swear that no one before has ever roused my vitals as you are doing now. Oh, blessed be the hour that you took it into your head to seek lodging in my poor abode!"

"Amen to that, my hospitable daughter," Father Lawrence rapturously agreed. "And now that I have regained my full composure, prepare yourself to feel the end of my blade within that marvelously narrow chink of yours!"

Eager to keep his word, the English ecclesiastic ground his teeth and thrust manfully forward, while at the same time distracting his naked landlady by continuing to fondle her panting breast and to frig her turgid clitoris. Hortense Bernard writhed lasciviously, uttering one sobbing little cry after another, yet stoically she did not avoid his vigorous charge but thrust back her naked hips so that he might harpoon her fundament to the very hilt. Thus he felt against his belly the shuddering, wriggling globes of her opulent backside, and his face turned purple with contorted lubricity as he called upon all his reserve powers to withhold the deluge of love-juice which yearned to burst forth without more delay.

His forefinger speeded its perorations against her dainty nodule, and augmented Hortense Bernard's furious responses. Her fingers clawed the sheets, her face turned restlessly from side to side, and he felt the naked breast within his cupping hand jut and rasp its swollen nipple bud against his palm as evidence of her fervent attonement.

Now he began to work his mighty weapon in and out of that protestingly contracting passage and the naked young widow squirmed and twisted herself this way and that as if to disengorge herself of the spear that was decimating her bowels. But in truth this was the last thing in the world she wished for (if I am to judge by her babbled supplications and whimperingly sobbed-out cries). "Ahhhrrr! Oh, faster, harder, Your Reverence! Ahh, your finger is driving me near to swooning—oh, oh, hold it back, Your Reverence, till I am ready too! Deeper, harder into me, I implore you—oh, what bliss, what joy you bring me!"

His forefinger flattened the stiffened tidbit of her clitoris back into its dainty little cowl of pink flesh, then let it bob up in all its glory; then he rubbed it from side to side, then pressed it down only to let it spring up again. By these sly means, he drew her ever closer towards the abyss of passion into which the hot and tight and squeezing enclaspment of her rectal walls against his imbedded ramrod threatened to plunge him at any instant. Finally, sensing from her quaking spasms and the tireless wriggling of her velvety, naked hips that she was almost at a fever pitch, he called out to her to accompany him on this flight into the empyrean. Then, with two or three violent eviscerating digs of his bursting weapon, he flooded her bowels with a deluge of hot viscous fluid even as her own mossy nook gave down its creamy libation to his delving forefinger. In her spasm, the comely widow's arms and legs gave way beneath her and she sprawled full length upon the bed with the good Father closely joined to her as they both gasped out their ecstasy.

And thus the visiting English ecclesiastic took up his new domicile and at the same time consoled the secretive burning desire of the frustrated and beautiful Widow Bernard.

CHAPTER ELEVEN

True to his promise, Père Mourier read the banns of the forthcoming marriage between Laurette Boischamp and Monsieur Claude Villiers that very next Sunday. Laurette and her parents sat in one pew, and the tender golden-haired virgin lowered her eyes and bowed her head in so maidenly downcast an attitude as to win favor even with her strict and upright parents. As for the worthy patron, seated in a pew opposite his bride-to-be and his intended in-laws, he stole covert glances at the luscious young virgin who was destined for his bed. He had but ten days to wait.

I promised myself to attend the lovely virgin Laurette and do my best to protect her in her hour of greatest peril. I felt a strangely compassionate sympathy for her, so soon to be linked to this scrawny, miserly and peevish old man.

In the church that same Sunday, seated in the same pew, were Dame Lucille and her good man, Jacques Tremoulier, and Dame Margot and her faithful Guillaume Noirceau. During Père Mourier's sermon, which had to do with St. Paul's maxim that it was better to marry than to burn, I caught the two wives stealing glances from time to time at the two sturdy husbands. I noted that Lucille and Guillaume exchanged as many meaningful glances as did Margot and Jacques; hence I concluded in the time that had elapsed since I had paid a visit to their cottages, the two couples had ably managed to trade consorts and spouses in a way that left them still amicably good neighbors and the best of friends. So I had been right in concluding that they did not need any assistance in working out their little destinies. But then, they were mature women mated to virile and broad-minded men, whereas poor Laurette had been deprived of the young swain who should have been the one to bed her and to give warm nature what it surely required instead of being forced to accept the bony, doubtless impotent, carcass of the patron as her legal bedfellow.

It is said that happy should be the bride who marries under the shining sun, and in truth the Wednesday of Laurette's union with the patron of Languecuisse was a gloriously sunny, pleasantly warm day that drew all the villagers to Père Mourier's church to witness the ceremony.

Laurette walked down the aisle on the arm of her father. He was in his best suit; she, with her two golden braids falling to her waist, wore a humble cotton gown, with a long skirt hiding her dainty ankles. The skirt flared out widely from her hips, no doubt due to some kind of hoop that disguised all the tempting young charms hidden under it. Her lovely blue eyes were red and swollen, for she had been weeping. She still mourned her lover, Pierre Laurrieu—I say her lover in spirit only, for you will recall that the unfortunate Pierre was thwarted at the most critical moment when he had hoped to pillage her maidenhead away from its lawfully intended possessor. Yes, she had been faithful to the ordainment which both Père Mourier and Father Lawrence had imposed upon her: to hold no converse or meeting with the young rogue and to save herself chastely for Monsieur Claude Villiers.

I could hear her mother scolding her in whispers

amid the bustle and the hum which prefaced the holy ceremony. Madame Boischamp was vexed that her daughter should put on so mournful and lugubrious a face on this, the most glorious day of her entire young life. At one fell swoop little Laurette was to become a great lady, the consort of the saviour of the village itself; yet she wept. Was there ever a more unreasonable wench? It was only maternal pride, and, to be sure, the greedy thoughts of how she and her husband would benefit from their own new status as relatives by marriage to Monsieur Villiers, that had kept Madame Boischamp from taking a hickory switch to Laurette's tender virgin backside before the wedding.

The ceremony did not last long, and after the villagers had poured out into the churchyard, the beaming patron, in a drab black suit which made him look more a scarecrow than ever, joyously proclaimed that there would be wine and freshly baked bread and cheese distributed to everyone in Languecuisse. They were all to drink to his health and to wish him and his bride long life and many sons.

The cheer that went up drowned out many of the mocking and even scabrous jeers of the older women and the overworked and harassed elders, who wished Monsieur Villiers no joy whatsoever of his bride and who tauntingly predicted that he would leave her maidenhead intact despite all his efforts this night.

Laurette Villiers—for such was her name now—took tearful leave of her good parents, and it must be said somewhat to their credit that even Madame Boischamp softened her heart and sniffed as she bade her daughter be of good cheer and do her best to make the worthy patron a faithful and obedient wife. Then the elderly vintner helped his blushing bride into the little carriage and himself took hold of the reins and clacked the carriage whip so that the black mare might take them both safely back to his elegant house. Laurette looked back at the receding populace, straining her misty blue eyes for a last glimpse of the little cottage in which she had been born and which she was leaving as a maiden for the very last time. Tonight she would sleep in a splendid bed, and there would even be servants to do her bidding. But her heart was heavy, for she was undeniably thinking of what should befall her this night. From time to time, along the route, the patron glanced covetously at his tender young bride, his eyes narrowing and glittering. I perched upon his top hat and looked sympathetically down at the sweet, heart-shaped, woefully saddened face of poor little Laurette. And all the compassion that is innate within the soul of a Flea was heavy within me.

At the door of Monsieur Villiers' elaborate mansion—for such it was in comparison to the humble cottages of his tenant farmers and vineyard workers—his housekeeper received them both. Her name was Victorine Dumady, and her face was downcast, too, out of spite and jealousy. She had been the patron's housekeeper for five years and she had just reached her fortieth birthday. Seeing the charming young bride, she now knew that all her hope of ensnaring the patron had fled. I had heard gossip enough from the villagers about this wily Victorine. Her face was homely, with the hint of a moustache on her upper lip, but her body was almost as voluptuously robust as that of Desirée. And she had used that body many a time to attempt to seduce the elderly patron into marriage. He had been, rumor had it, as impotent with her as with many damsels of tenderer age. He had proved with none of them that he was still a virile cocksmith.

He made the introduction of his new bride to Victorine with a certain sneering braggadocio, as much as to imply to her: "Do you not see what a toothsome young morsel I have brought to warm my bed? How can you dare expect me to content myself with worn-out goods like you, discriminating roué that I am?"

But Laurette, with that intuition with which all females are apparently blessed, must have sensed the rancor in Victorine's heart, for she sweetly greeted the robust matron with a tender kiss upon the forehead and a promise that, since her own knowledge of domesticity was so slight, she would never dare assert her will on Victorine as to the management of the kitchen or the household. Further, she asked if she might be shown to her room so that she might rest a little while, because the excitement of the ceremony and the parting from her parents had overwhelmed her.

Victorine's sour face at once brightened and very tenderly she put an arm about Laurette's shoulders and gently offered to show her to her new chamber. Glancing back at her master, she added somewhat tartly, "You must allow Madame a little time to compose herself, Sir, or you will have no joy with her tonight."

The chamber to which Laurette was taken was across the hall from that in which her virginity would be forfeit this very night. There was a little bed, a table with a mirror, a chest of drawers, and a spacious closet for the clothes the patron had promised his new bride. Laurette sighed as she inspected the elegant room with its shutters and its fine rug, such a far cry from the earthen floor of the humble little cottage where she had first seen the light of day. Then, her emotions overcoming her, she put her hands to her face and began to weep silently. Victorine was touched. "Come now, Madame, it will not be so bad," she soothed the charming virgin. "Now that my own hope of gaining the rank you now hold is no more, I can be honest with you, my pretty child. His bark is worse than his bite, and his hopes are more valiant than his deeds when it comes to bedding a wench. I am more than twice your age, Madame, but he cannot even service me. You need have no fear, therefore. Oh, it is true that you will have to show your lovely person naked to him, but I wager that it will excite him so much that he will not even be able to break your hymen. Now lie down and calm yourself, and I shall presently bring you a little cordial."

"You—you are very kind, Victorine," Laurette faintly murmured.

"Not by nature, truly, Madame Villiers," the robust matron candidly retorted, with a shrug of her ripe, round shoulders, "but I am a practical woman and, as you may well guess, I have had to put up with his foibles for several years. I know him as well as I know the back of my own hand. So do not fret. Tell yourself only that you must be brave for a little time when the bony old fool wishes to exact payment for having given you his name in holy matrimony."

With this encouraging piece of advice, Victorine left the room, and Laurette flung herself on the bed and sobbed aloud over having been separated from Pierre Larrieu for what assuredly at this moment seemed forever.

I need not dwell upon the wedding supper which Victorine was obliged to serve, nor expatiate on the ludicrous and risible manner of the patron, who fancied himself to be very cavalier with the ladies and made all sorts of ribald and lewd quips on the approaching moment when he should be alone with his bride for the first time. Laurette, though a gentle virgin, was, as I have tried to imply already, a wise virgin also; she understood many of these bawdy references, though she pretended to be impervious to them. She toyed with her food, although it was the richest fare she had ever been privileged to sup upon, all in the hope of delaying that inexorable and inevitable hour. By contrast, however, she did help herself to three glasses of good Burgundy and two more of fine champagne, which Victorine served. I do not know whether her mother had counseled her to seek solace in alcoholic spirits, just as criminals condemned to the guillotine are often permitted absinthe to dull their terrors of execution. But I have no doubt that she imbibed these stimulants in the hope of making the forthcoming juncture between herself and the patron a less agonizing obligation.

Toward the end of the repast, I found it hard to check my own hilarity when I heard Monsieur Villiers ask several times in his querulous voice, "Aren't you fatigued, my dear? Wouldn't you like to go to bed now?" In his role as patron of the village, having the droit de seigneur privilege over every damsel and matron in Languecuisse, it was not mandatory upon him to show the amorous gallantry of a courtier, for this, after all, was a simple peasant village in the heart of Provence. Nonetheless, a child could have seen through his bald hints, and Laurette did her level best to evade the issue. Victorine was a close ally in this regard, seeing to it that the new Madame Villiers had another little helping of mousse or another mint or another demitasse while the unprepossessing visage of the patron grew steadily dark as a thundercloud as his patience waned and his impatience to be at naked oneness with his tasty young virgin bride increased.

But finally there was no help for it: Laurette had taken the last morsel of food and the last sip of champagne that she could stomach, and now, alas, she had to stomach the patron himself. She finally rose, her face blushing in her sweet bridal confusion, and the old fool shoved back his chair and scurried to her to take her arm with his bony fingers and to declare in his ready voice, "Lean on me, my little pigeon. I shall conduct you to the nuptial chamber myself. You will see how tenderly I will care for you, my darling Laurette. You do not know how I have waited for this moment!"

Had he let it go at that the old fool might possibly have roused in Laurette some vague tolerance of her elderly benedict. But the habits of a lifetime are difficult to curb. And, sure enough, no sooner had they passed the threshold of the dining room, he surreptitiously pinched her tender bottom. Laurette started, turned scarlet, and uttered a gasp. She gazed at her husband reproachfully, two big tears forming in those glorious soft blue eyes. The patron of Languecuisse cackled with ribald merriment: "Eh, eh, my beauty, you did not think I was so spry at my age, I'll wager. I will surprise you this night, my plump little pigeon. You will fall back on your pillow and beg for mercy, I promise you. I will make you forget that rascally Pierre Larrieu before the sun rises in the heavens, of that you may be certain. Come, my little beauty, come to bed!"

Laurette allowed herself to be conducted to the bridal chamber. With ill-concealed lubricity, the patron flung open the door and triumphantly pointed towards the canopied four-poster bed, which rose so imposingly and menacingly before the tender eyes of this beautiful peasant virgin. "Is that bed not magnificent, my dear little Laurette?" he cackled. "There are two mattresses, and they are packed with eiderdown to cradle your lovely flesh. Come, give me a tender kiss before you disrobe, a kiss that will tell me you are mine at last, my exquisite little pigeon!"

Laurette dutifully put her hands on his shoulders, closed her eyes, and gave him a peck on the cheek, which did not at all please him. "But that is no kiss at all, you teasing little vixen," he snorted. "Do you not know that I am your proper husband now, with every right over you? You must obey my every wish, Laurette. That is the law and Père Mourier will tell you your duties if you do not know them already." With this, he crushed his thin, dry lips upon her rosy mouth, and Laurette winced and shuddered, wishing that some miracle might whisk her away from this gaudy bedchamber and take her instead to a hayrick wherein she might lie naked in the embrace of her sturdy, loving Pierre.

But, alas, it was not to be.

Laurette, realizing that the frightful hour was here at last and that no one would break in to save her, not even her adored Pierre, blushingly petitioned her elderly husband to let her disrobe in privacy. But the patron was not to be put off so deviously. "Ah, no, my little pigeon," he slyly retorted, "I will not let you out of my sight till I have had you and properly enjoyed your maiden treasure, which is my due because you are now my bride! I know your scheme, you sweet trickster, aye, I know it well. You would slip off to your room, promising to change into your nightshift, and then I should find you fled out to the fields with this rascally bastard who would usurp all my privileges!"

"Oh, no, no, Monsieur Villiers, how can you think such a thing of me? I am a good girl, a virgin, and I am dying of shame to think that now I-I must take off my clothes and—and let you see me. At least, send Victorine in to me to help me prepare for bed."

"There is no need for that, my beauty," he greedily parried her last ruse. "As your husband, I will act as your maid this eve. And there is no need for shame now, my little pigeon, since we are man and wife. Come, quickly, take off your gown. I am longing to see your beautiful white skin again, remembering how you looked in the wine cask when I let you win the contest!"

"Oh, M'sieu, then I do not belong here this night at your side," Laurette ingeniously countered, employing every resource in her power to stop the odious consummation from taking place. "I did not think my cask was as full of grapes as the others. It was unfair and I should not have been the winner. You should rightly wed her who squeezed out the most liters."

"Enough of this time-wasting argument, my beauty," Claude Villiers growled. "If you will not undress by yourself I will rip your garments from you. I am within my rights. Verily, I may even thrash you with a switch if you are not a properly obedient wife to me. It is the law, Laurette."

The frightened girl raised her beautiful, teary eyes to the ceiling and falteringly began to remove her gown while the scrawny bridegroom watched, rubbing his bony hands with anticipation. Beneath the gown, she wore a camisole, petticoat, and drawers, as well as white clockwork stockings, secured on her lower thighs with blue satin rosette garters. Her dainty feet were shod in little shoes with brass buckles. Claude Villiers licked his lips and his voice cracked with feverish anticipation as he ordered, "And now the petticoat, my pretty one."

"Oh, please, M'sieu Villiers, I-I have never undressed before in front of a man. Will you not let me go into the next room and put on my nightdress?" Laurette stammered.

"No, my darling pet! As to a nightdress, there is no need for it, because it would only come off anyway," he cackled. Then, his eyes narrowing suspiciously, "Do not waste any more time by arguing with me, girl! The petticoat!"

Laurette's dainty little fingers fumbled with the string that held the petticoat snugly about her slim waist and at last managed to loosen the knot. The garment fluttered down to her ankles, and she stepped out of it, an entrancing vision in her camisole, drawers and the snugly sheathing white stockings.

"Now the camisole," he directed, licking his dry, thin lips again, his beady little eyes bright with the unholy glow of inordinate lust.

"Oh, S-sir," Laurette quavered, "won't you at least put out the candles? I shall faint away of shame if I must strip all n-naked before you. I am innocent and—and afraid."

"Which is precisely what makes you so deliciously tempting, you darling little pigeon," Claude Villiers cackled. "Take comfort in my impatient desire for your charms, my beauty, for I would not be half so excited if I had been told that you had lain with another man."

This statement somewhat eased Laurette's fears, for she had dreaded the possibility that Père Mourier had informed the elderly patron of what had almost transpired between herself and Pierre Larrieu on that grassy knoll the evening after the grape-trampling contest. It gave her courage once again to formulate a chaste entreaty: "Oh, Sir, it is just because I have no knowledge whatsoever of a man's desire that I beg you humbly to take pity on my tender modesty and not to force me to that which my good parents have brought me up to regard as sinful and immodest."

"Your estimable parents have taught you well, my little pigeon. It is right that a virgin keep herself chaste for her wedding night. But your hour has arrived and I, by right of the ceremony this afternoon which made us one, have the sole privilege of exposing all your luscious charms and enjoying them to the fullest. Therefore you, being my wife, must obey my smallest whims, and I now insist that you to take off the camisole without further delay!"

Laurette bit her lips and flushed hotly as the

patron's eyes fixed her with a greedily lustful stare. Finally, she yielded to circumstance, and, shyly turning to one side, took hold of the thin garment and drew it over head and shoulders, letting it fall to the floor. She quickly covered her milky bosom with both arms. A tremulous, wistful sob escaped her as she thought of her absent lover, to whom she would gladly have made every conceivable sacrifice.

Panting with excitement at the notion that his tender young bride wore only drawers and hose, the elderly patron began to divest himself of his clothing and finally stood stark naked. His bony shanks, his shrunken chest—the emaciated paps of which were hidden by patches of whitesh hair—his bony arms and the almost obscene baldness of his skull, made Laurette's sweet eyes widen in revulsion. But most of all, the sight of his dwindled, shriveled cock and the hairy gnarled, egg-shaped balls, informed her most glaringly of his impotence as compared with the rugged young virility of the blond youth who had nearly plucked her flower of chastity.

"Come, put your milky arms around my neck, my charming pigeon," he panted, "and kiss your husband as is mete and seemly on this night of our nuptials! Your maidenly confusion is understandable and does your chastity credit, but now that we are alone with none to intrude on or endanger your sweet secrets, prepare yourself to give up all these maidenly vapors!"

I pitied Laurette with all my heart as I watched her timidly approach the grotesquely naked, grinning old vintner. As her rounded, milky arms hesitantly wound themselves about his withered neck, I caught sight of the glorious firm rondures of her virgin bosom, the soft coral darts of her sweet nipples. To think that such charms must be sacrificed upon so unworthy an altar was odious indeed; Monsieur Claude Villiers was old enough to be, not Laurette's father, but her grandfather. It was—this intended mating—somewhat akin to incest. And even when her milky breasts shudderingly pressed against his shrunken chest, his dwindled cock paid not the least tribute to such voluptuous young beauty.

"How soft and sweet you are," he panted as his hands tremblingly roved over her bare, smooth, satiny white back and thence to the succulent hemisphere of her enticing virgin backside, which I had already seen naked under the scourge of Père Mourier. "You can't know how I've longed to see and feel your nakedness, Laurette! When the good Father told me that you were taken with a seizure the night of the contest, I grieved in my dire loneliness. I felt such a loss that I very nearly summoned that bold jade, the Widow Desirée, to console me. So would I have done had I not been told by your good Father confessor that he had only just that day engaged her as his very own housekeeper."

I liked this old man less and less after that bragging, tasteless speech. However, I understood his motive: He was fearful for his own severe lack of cocksmanship, and now, confronted by so voluptuous a beauty, was desirous of impressing on her innocent mind the belief that he was a vaunted lover to whose bedchamber would come the most passionate wenches in Languecuisse. I vowed to myself to protect Laurette's tender maidenhead to the utmost, so far as it was within my tiny powers.

"S-sir," Laurette quavered, "please, l-let me go this first night. I-I promise I will try my best to be a faithful wife to you, but I am so lonely and despondent at being separated from my dear parents that I cannot find it in my heart to grant you that which you desire of me."

Monsieur Claude Villiers sniggered at this poetic and poignant declaration. His bony fingers had by now taken hold of the poutingly rounded hemispheres of Laurette's resilient, virgin backside, and he was in no way desirous of relinquishing his fair prize. "Nay, nay, my sweet pigeon, I will be both father and mother to you tonight. And somewhat more, eh, eh!" Then, his face flushed and, hardening with angry desire, he commended, "Now I wish to see you with your drawers off, my beauty! All that you possess is now mine, to see, to feel, to caress as I desire! Be quick now!"

Tears ran down Laurette's milky cheeks as she recoiled, her arms once again hiding her panting naked bosom. "Oh, Sir, I know I must obey you, but will you not have pity on my unhappiness and at least blow out the candles? I-I will kiss you as sweetly as I can, and sleep beside you, but give me a few days to accustom myself to your wants, I beg you humbly!"

Such a supplication, needless to say, only inflamed the old lecher all the more. He seized her by the wrist and pulled her towards the huge, ornate bed, gasping, "You shall do more than sleep, my girl! You belong to me, every part of you, and I mean to enjoy my possession! I mean to fuck you gloriously this night!"

Thereupon, he flung her down onto the bed, and grabbing at the hem of her thin drawers, whisked them off as one would skin a rabbit, flinging the offending garment to the floor. The beautiful milky-skinned, golden-haired Laurette was naked save for her hose and shoes! These, too, he removed and then stood looking down at her, his eyes shining pinpoints of licentiousness, while the tender maiden, bursting into tears, clapped one soft hand over her virgin cunt hole and with the other arm did her best to hide the lovely round turrets of her maiden teats. "Oh, have mercy, M'sieu Villiers," she whimpered.

He clambered into bed beside her and the sweet

virgin promptly rolled onto one side to evade him, turning her beautifully sculptured, satiny back and luscious, velvety bottom cheeks to him. Panting with lust, the patron cuddled up to her spoon-fashion, his right hand gliding up her thigh and over to the golden furred mount of her maiden cunny, while she tried to protect that very spot by clamping her soft, trembling little palm over that diadem of chastity. Excited by the satiny feel of her warm, quivering naked flesh, the elderly reprobate began to rub his dwindled cock against the plump hemispheres of Laurette's shivering bare bottom. I saw Laurette's eyes close, a grimace of disgust contorting her heart-shaped, sweet face.

"You are angering me with your obstinacy, girl," he warned. "Take care or I will give you a sound thrashing to teach you your duties to your husband!"

"Oh, have pity, Sir," Laurette stammered, huddling herself with all her muscular exertion and frantically preventing his groping fingers from reaching the sacrosanct niche of her maiden cunt hole. "You—you must give me time to know what you wish of me—oh, do not force me, I implore you, if you wish me to have the least affection for you!"

But the friction of her voluptuous, naked bottom against his emaciated weapon had wrought a veritable miracle; Monsieur Claude Villiers was now in a state of tolerable erection. His cock was not much longer than five inches, and the long, thin head seemed to droop slightly, yet I could see by the spasmodic jerkings of his gnarled balls that he was in a condition of fair erotic excitement.

As she showed no sign of turning towards him, but continued to huddle herself in almost a fetal pose, one arm pressed over her tumultuously swelling titties, the other little hand clamped tightly over the plump mound of her cunt, the patron then cast what little compassion he had to the four winds and with an angry imprecation, seized her by the shoulders and forcibly turned her onto her back. Then, feverishly panting with exertion, he flung himself down on her, kneeing apart her palpitating thighs and rubbing the drooping head of his pitiful tool against the furry, golden ringlets which now provided her sole defense against his intended rape. Laurette, with a cry of alarm, tried to push at him with her soft little hands but she was at an obvious disadvantage because he had managed to fit himself into her saddle.

It was time for me to lend my aid to this beleaguered virgin. Seeing my chance, I hopped from the counterpane—he had not even bothered to turn down the sheets in his inopportune fury for the conquest of her sweet maiden cunt—and nimbly leapt between their bodies just as poor Laurette managed to wriggle slightly out from under her elderly ravisher. I crawled onto his left testicle and applied my proboscis. He uttered a shrill cry of pain, for I had bitten deeply, and rolled off the sobbing, naked maiden, rubbing his hurt. I, of course, foreseeing this, had already left him for a place of greater safety.

My intervention had come at an excellent moment: already his cock was flaccid and completely drooping between his shriveled, bony thighs. He glared at Laurette as if it were entirely her fault that he was put temporarily out of commission.

"Ventre-Saint-Gris!" he swore malevolently, still rubbing his throbbing testicle, "I am out of patience with your silly tears and chaste airs, my pigeon! Do you wish me to summon my overseer, Hercule, to apply the switch to your impertinent backside and then hold you down while I take my rights?"

"Oh, no, no, Sir, do not treat me so cruelly! Oh, be kind, M'sieu Villiers," she whimpered, her blue eyes blinded by tears.

"I have but to reach my hand to the bellpull

beside the bed," he warned, gesturing to it with his free hand, "and I will do so this moment unless you submit yourself docilely." He made he made as if to reach for it and Laurette uttered a woebegone cry: "Oh, stop! I-I will submit!"

"That's better," he growled, his crest heaving with the effect of this heated struggle for that soft, golden-thatched jewel which hid between Laurette's milky, rounded thighs. "Then pillow your head on your soft arms, my pigeon, spread your thighs lovingly, and prepare to receive me!"

Closing her eyes and turning her face to one side, poor little Laurette reluctantly obeyed. Licking his lips again, the vile old lecher crawled upon her trembling milky-skinned nakedness. Ugh, it was like seeing some bloodsucking leech profane a lily! His bony fingers set to work pinching and prodding her shuddering bare bubbies, and his thin dry lips nuzzled the valley between those round proud young globes, whilst he rasped his dormant cock against the furry fronds of her maiden mount in an effort to restore himself to that happy, if accidental, vigour with he had enjoyed before my intervention.

His mouth now besieged the soft coral tip of one beautiful, shuddering breast and sucked it as if hoping that by this means he might draw nourishment enough to fortify his puerile virility. Great tears edged from under Laurette's eyelids at this desecration.

Now his bony fingers reached under Laurette's squirming backside and gouged the milky, succulent young flesh as he hastened the obscene grinding of his limp cock against the silky pussy fur of his virginal bride in a frantic effort to become adequate for her defloration. The charming girl had turned her face to one side and the cords of her soft, round neck were taunt and standing out against the milky white skin—evidence of her great aversion to her pathetic despoiler. Yet gradually once again, thanks to the warm sweet contact of Laurette's maiden mount against his atrophied organ, Monsieur Claude Villiers managed to attain a second erection, though not nearly so virile as the first. And once again it was time for me to intervene on her behalf. As he raised himself up on his bony, shaking knees, his flushed face gazing down hungrily at the sight of her tumultuously swelling, naked breasts, I hopped to his scrotum and gave him a wicked little nip which caused him to utter a hoarse yell and to invoke the aid of Satan himself as he stared abjectly down at his once-again diminished cock, utterly useless for the fray that he had intended.

"Ohh, f-finish it, S-sir, I pray you," Laurette's voice came faintly, "before I die of shame!"

"A thousand fiends upon this luckless night," he swore. "Whether it is your bewitching white skin or its softness that destroys me, I cannot achieve my way and fuck you as you deserve, my lovely little pigeon! I would sell my soul to Lucifer could he but invigorate me to the shattering of your chaste virgin seal! Ah, but there is another way by which you may avow your fealty to me, your rightful lord and master! And, by the eternal, you shall forthwith demonstrate it!"

With this, he flung himself down on his back beside her, and, cupping her trembling chin in his scrawny hand, hissed, "Kneel over me and put your sweet red lips to my prick and draw forth the essence I have saved up so long for you, which was better destined for your adorable little cunt but which some demonic force has balked."

I was almost inclined to bite him a third time at such an insult, for I am not and never have been leagued with the Lord of Evil, even though it may be the opinion of some misguided scholars that a plague of fleas was sent to pester Job as one of his many trials.

"Oh—M'sieu, I-I do not quite understand what it

is you would have me do," the tender maiden stammered, but I saw the telltale suffusion of her blushes spread to her dainty little ears and soft, pulsing throat.

"Mon dieu, but you cannot be such an innocent," he growled. Then, pointing to his dwindled weapon, he explicitly commanded: "You will take my cock between your lips and suck me till my juices spurt into your mouth and down your lovely throat. There, do you at last comprehend me?"

"Ohh! How—how can you ask me to perform such a vile task?" Laurette gasped.

"Because, you maddening creature, you must satisfy me one way or another tonight, and, since ill chance prevents my thrusting my cock into your cunny, your mouth must substitute. Obey me, or I swear I shall have Hercule flog you smartly!"

"Ohhh, heavens!" Laurette sobbed, "I am helpless, Sir, I cannot resist such brute force. V-very well, then, I-I will try to obey you, but it will make me faint, I am sure!"

"Nonsense, it did not make Desirée faint," he panted, and crawled over her, turning himself so that his loins were directly over her scarlet, tearstained face, while he in turn faced the quaking, clenching columns of her milky round thighs and the adorable, golden-thatched nook which they sequestered. Lowering himself, he brushed the tip of her dainty nose with the wrinkled, drooping head of his cock, and gasped, "Quickly, open your lips and pay homage to your husband!"

Laurette sighed woefully as she resigned herself. I could not read her virgin mind, and yet I was sure that she was weighing the relatively less odious compliance of performing fellatio on him against the umbrage of submitting to the shattering of her maiden seal by his senile cock. At least in this way she would cherish her virginity for her true lover, Pierre Larrieu, and still be faithful to him even as a bride of this elderly and detestable vintner.

So, keeping her eyes tightly closed, she reluctantly opened her rosy lips and absorbed the dwarfed shriveled stick of her senile husband, who at once uttered a cry of ecstasy: "Ahhh, that is heavenly! Now suck it gently and slowly, and entwine your soft fingers over my thighs—yes, that's it—ohh, I am in heaven! And you will discover, my white-skinned beauty, that in due time I shall be able to fuck your cunny as it merits, once you and I are intimately acquainted with each other as true spouse and consort should always be!"

Her beautiful, shapely thighs were tightly clutched together to deny him the least access, but Monsieur Claude Villiers did not have any generous impulses in his hour of lust, and so he did not even try to caress her cunny with his fingers, much less gamahuche her as reward for her sweet oral ministrations. I liked him less and less with each passing moment. Even the two bites I had taken granted me very little blood and less nourishment, he being dried-up and inconsequential as regards provender for me just as he was in bringing fruition to the loins of this sweet virgin who lay naked upon his lordly bed.

His groans and squirmings attested, however, to his approaching climax: I did not know whether gentle Laurette was sufficiently endowed by her female intuition to be aware of this imminent gush of viscous spunk, but I considered its emission into so fair an orifice far more than the senile patron deserved.

So, just as his rolling eyes and heaving chest and flanks demonstrated the very imminence of his little moment, I hopped from the pillow to the middle of his shaft and inflicted my third and sharpest bite, which caused him to utter a frenzied cry and roll off the startled naked girl. Clapping both hands to his throbbing cock, he succeeded in drenching his own bony fingers with the defiling spunk instead of flooding into Laurette's still-virgin mouth.

Defeated and undone, Monsieur Claude Villiers sulkily lay beside the apprehensive maiden, who had nothing more to fear from him this night. For presently his snores told her, as they did me, that she was still an untarnished bride. Yet her dulcet sighs and wrigglings for the rest of the night suggested that, in her radiant dreams, the virile, young Pierre Laurrieu was accomplishing that which her own husband had not done.

CHAPTER TWELVE

After a week, Laurette's maidenhead was still intact. I was a witness to the two more futile attempts which Monsieur Claude Villiers essayed against the golden-haired maiden's virtue. The first of these followed on the night after her marriage and it took a comic turn very much like that which I have already described to my readers. The old fool had fortified himself with some powerful cognac after dinner, having told his bride to await him in the nuptial chamber while he sat at his ease in his salon smoking a good cigar and sipping the fiery spirits. Just to make certain that he would be adequate this time, he actually opened his trousers and began to play with his dwindled organ so as to bring it to a state of competence before entering the bridal chamber.

Laurette had docilely disrobed and was awaiting him, meek as a sacrificial lamb upon that great bed. This time, however, she had found a nightshift which fitted her passably well, evidently a garment worn by one or another of the patron's many mistresses. When he entered he frowned to see that her white flesh was not at once displayed in all its gleaming beauty, for that would have been a further stimulant to his lustfulness. But, resolutely determined to breach the walls of the thus-far impregnable castle of her chastity, he undressed himself and once again stood ludicrously naked before the tender maiden. He immediately hastened to clamber upon her and rub himself against her grudging loins. I waited nearby to determine whether again to make him fall short of the mark, but this time I did not need to. His excitement was so great in feeling the sweet silken friction of her cunny hairs against his throbbing, yet still-meager lance that he shot his bolt, spattering her round sweet belly before he could even lodge the head of his tool between the pouting soft pink lips.

So, once again his cock had recourse to her mouth, under threat of a flogging. And once again the farcical comedy went to its very end, with Laurette grimacing and closing her eyes and allowing her rosy lips to take hold of his detestable weapon. But, work on it as she would—and her performance was somewhat longer this time because of his angry insistence—she could not succeed in making him reach the state of rigidity that was desired. He had to lie beside her and fall asleep, content with his scurrilous dreams.

The next attempt was made four days later, and this time the old fool gave her a stern order to await him naked as the day she was born upon the nuptial bed. When he entered, he carried with him some lengths of felt cord which he proceeded to wrap around her wrists and ankles. He then fixed these to the bedposts, thereby leaving her spread-eagled in the most vulnerable and lascivious way conceivable.

Laurette began to weep and beg him not to ravage her by force, for that way, she quavered, would only make her detest him and not at all respect his husbandly status. But this appeal fell on deaf ears as the patron greedily mounted the huge bed and knelt between poor Laurette's straining, yawning thighs. His hands this time lasciviously roved over her defenseless body, pinching her breasts and belly and hips and thighs till she squealed and squirmed. At least he managed a kind of half-potency and made haste to fling himself down upon her, his scrawny chest flattening her shuddering, milky bubbies and his thin, dry lips stifling the cry that rose from her sweet, rosy mouth.

I believed then that Laurette was in the most terrible danger of all, but again I had reckoned without the intervention of demanding nature. So keen had been his anticipation of pillaging her treasure in this fettered and helpless condition that he again ejaculated his seed before it could reach inside her matrix. Just as the tip of his cock prodded between the tender lips of Laurette's virgin cunny, his eyes rolled in his head and his face turned a fiery red and this time his premature burst sullied her inner thighs and lower belly.

She was once again constrained to service him with her mouth, but the effort was useless as he was again rendered impotent. Grumpily he flung himself down beside her without even bothering to release her bonds, and so fell asleep, ignoble and selfish wretch that he was.

During the interim between these two occasions when Monsieur Villiers sought to have sexual congress with his tender young bride, I made my way back to the little cottage of the Widow Bernard on one evening and to the rectory of Père Mourier on another occasion. As it chanced, the fat French priest had been summoned to the parish of Jardineannot, about a dozen kilometers to the west, to perform the funeral service for a dear old friend. As a consequence Father Lawrence, telling his buxom landlady that he had been requested to substitute for Père Mourier in the event that the villagers of Languecuisse might need spiritual consolation during the latter's absence, made a nocturnal visit to the little rectory. There he found the beautiful Amazonian housekeeper, Desirée, alone and ecstatically eager to give him further proof of her burning devotion. She prepared a tasty meal for him, adding even a bottle of Père Mourier's best wine, and the two of them ate and drank with gusto. When they had finished he sighed, sated, and avowed that he would not be able to move for hours after so filling a repast.

The beautiful widow roguishly told him that she would not disturb him for all the world, yet his immobility need not impair their enjoyment. As he leaned back in the straight-backed chair, Desirée divested herself of her skirt and this time of her drawers also, for not knowing of this delightful visit from the virile English ecclesiastic, she had not been nakedly prepared. Next, lofting his cassock and lowering his drawers, she seated herself with her back to him, her legs straddling over his, and, reaching between her boldly yawning thighs, took hold of his already prodigiously excited spear and drew it towards her furry niche. Her sighs and gasps of delight evidenced the unusually stimulating angle with which his cock rasped against her inner channel, granting her indescribable pleasure. By dint of squirming about and arching gently and then lowering herself, she was able to bring them both to the most heavenly state of erotic rapture.

And when they had both rested from this delightful pursuit of carnal gratification, she led him into the bedroom of Père Mourier and there they renewed—with fiery vigor and enthusiasm—their fleshly union. I witnessed two exciting bouts, the first of which took place with Father Lawrence firmly mounted over his beautiful and passionate steed, whereas the second foray was accomplished with Desirée kneeling on all fours and the apparently tireless holy man behind her and foraging his sturdy weapon deep within her cunny.

On the other occasion, Father Lawrence showed that he was not at all unmindful of the debt he owed the Widow Bernard for her tender hospitality. He crept into her bedchamber after she had gone to sleep, only to find her tossing and turning restlessly and murmuring incoherent words. Drawing off the thin sheets, for it was another warm night, he tickled the lips of her cunny and her clitoris until he wakened her. Thus exquisitely attended, she uttered a cry of joy and held out her arms to him. He possessed her lingeringly. Midway through their juncture, he obliged her to draw her knees up against her sumptuous bosom, and then, taking hold of the backs of her knees, directed himself deeply into her moist and quaking love-channel.

On the Thursday afternoon which marked the start of the second week of poor Laurette's marriage to the elderly patron, both Père Mourier and Father Lawrence conferred at the former's rectory on the subject of bringing this charming wench within their reach. It was decided that Père Mourier would pay a call this very evening on the excuse of bringing her to confession. He would gently remind the golden-haired young bride that it was high time she closet herself with her spiritual mentor and announce to him her new attitude on the subject of wifely obligations. Now Monsieur Villiers, angrily frustrated, as we well know, from not having perforated Laurette's coveted hymen, had decided to turn his attentions to his vineyards and to the bottling of the good wine from those grapes which had been harvested. Consequently, he spent the morning and afternoon out in the fields with his workers and with his overseer, Hercule, and gave his bride to understand that he would be thus occupied at least through the following week.

Having returned at sundown, exhausted from his unwonted physical labors, the patron went straight to his bedchamber and to sleep. So when Père Mourier was announced by the housekeeper, Victorine, he found charming Laurette alone in her own room, fully clothed and deliciously provocative as ever to his expertly appraising eyes.

"My daughter," he said unctuously, "it is high time that you make your confession. Will you not come to my rectory tomorrow afternoon so that this obligation may be fulfilled in complete privacy, as is befitting so grave a ceremony."

Laurette cast down her beautiful blue eyes and averred that she would keep the appointment. And so on Friday afternoon she made her way to the rectory and was smilingly received by the beautiful Desirée and ushered at once into the presence of the obese French priest.

But Laurette also found Father Lawrence seated at his ease near the little curtained booth into which she was to go. Père Mourier had had this second confession booth installed in his rectory, just off the salon, for special occasions, whereas most of his parishioners, naturally, avowed their sins in the church itself.

"Good day, Father," Laurette stammered, rather nervous at discovering that she would have to bare her secret heart to, not one, but two, Father confessors. "Do not be afraid, my child," Father Lawrence smilingly responded, "it is only that the worthy Père Mourier was gracious enough to invite me, a visitor from English shores, to observe what very close communication he keeps with his flock in this charming village. It may well be that I shall learn much from him to take back to England with me, and thereby spread more good. So go make a clean breast of your misdeeds and misthoughts, my daughter, and you will be heartened thereby."

So the golden-haired young beauty, mastering her embarrassment, entered the little confessional and knelt down on the cloth-covered rail, whilst Père Mourier made his way to the other side and began pompously: "I am ready now, my child, to hear your confession."

Laurette's soul was a tender and sweet one, I am certain. In the main she had not really much to confess in that short time which had elapsed between her last confession and her first week of marriage. Solely, she expressed deep regret that she had been forced to marry against her will, because she did not love her husband and was not sure that she ever could.

To this, Père Mourier assumed a highly sententious line of reasoning, reminding her that the Israelites, after escaping Egypt, remembered their sorrows and their tribulations for centuries thereafter by means of ceremonials. "Just so," he concluded, "you must realize that in return for your blessings and good things, you must pay the price of some small annoyances, for life is never perfect, my dear child."

"Alas, mon père," Laurette sighed, "I tell myself this daily, but it does not seem to ease the pangs in my grieving heart. I still mourn my Pierre."

"That is scandalous, my daughter. Satan himself lurks in the darkness, waiting to seize your mortal soul the moment you entertain thoughts of adulterous consorting. For such it is, and do not doubt it; now that you are wed in lawful estate to the good patron whose name you bear, it behooves you to remain as irreproachable as Caesar's wife herself. Try to remember that, my child."

"I-I will, mon père," Laurette quavered. She had doubtless thought herself finished with this painful interrogation when suddenly Père Mourier interposed: "Now, before I give you your penance, my daughter, you must tell me whether you have made every possible effort to be a good and obedient wife to your husband."

"Yes, mon père, I-I am sure that I have done my best," was the tremulous answer.

"Well, then, that is virtuous indeed—if it is so. But I would have a strict accounting from you, Laurette, as to this vital question: Have you humbly and truly granted your husband his conjugal rights? By this I mean, of course, have you permitted him access to your body that he may cleave unto you, as is prescribed by all the tenets of a good marriage?"

"I-I have gone to bed with him when—when he has wished it, yes, mon père," Laurette's voice trembled even more now, "but, and I do not know why, he—he has been unable to make love to me."

"What is this?" thundered the fat priest. "Do you mean that he has not yet taken your maidenhead?"

"N-no, mon père. But it was not for want of trying, I swear to you."

"That makes no difference. If you are still virgin it could only be because of your wicked resentment of the worthy patron and your clandestine and unholy lust for that scoundrel Pierre, whom you yearn to put in your husband's rightful place. This is sinfulness, my daughter, and must be chastised severely. I exhort you to see to it, this very night—aye, mark my words, Laurette!—that you bring your husband to a consummation of this marriage. Do you understand me? He is to take your hymen in the nuptial bed before the sun rises on the morrow. Then I bid you come to confessional tomorrow at one in the afternoon to relate to me whether you have fulfilled my ordainment. And woe betide your bottom, my rebellious child, if I find that you have not heeded my counsel. Now go back to the house of your husband and recite a hundred Hail Marys."

Laurette emerged from the confessional booth, her face streaked with tears, her eyes downcast, and she did not even give Father Lawrence a second glance as she left the rectory, her mind full of poignant anguish at the thought of the edict the fat French priest had laid upon her.

I had decided to remain in the salon to find out the reaction of these two worthy ecclesiastics, for I suspected that they themselves had designs upon this delicious virgin. Père Mourier had already shown as much in his lascivious scourging of her naked bottom. And, after having witnessed Father Lawrence's lusty fornicatory antics with the two beautiful widows, Desirée and Hortense, I felt him made of the same cloth as Père Mourier.

"You see, Father Lawrence, how stubborn the child is?" Père Mourier wagged a fat reproving finger, then he shook his head with a doleful sigh. "Lucifer wages a frightful struggle with me for the possession of her tender soul. If the two of us do not prevent her from casting aside her marital obligations and fleeing to the arms of that good-for-nothing, she will be damned to eternal perdition. And I do not mind telling you, in all confidence, Father Lawrence, that the worthy Monsieur Claude Villiers will at once cease his contributions to my little parish, which would leave me impoverished and unable to carry out the good works of faith which this so-often sinful village so desperately needs."

"I see your predicament, my confrère," the English ecclesiastic gravely agreed. "You shall have my aid, I pledge it. But how shall we constrain Laurette to keep her vows?"

"I have in mind a scheme that, while it is somewhat audacious, will surely prove successful. You overheard me telling the wench to see to it that her husband deflower her this very night? Well, why should we not make sure of this ourselves? He has been out to the vineyards all this week and will come home late in the evening. Let us, therefore, go to his abode and secrete ourselves in the closet of his bedchamber. Thence we can watch and behold Laurette's obedience or lack of it. And should she seek, once he falls asleep, to steal out of the house to her wretched lover, we shall be there to enforce her righteousness. You, being a foreign priest, will terrify her all the more by your authority, since she now knows that you and I are in league together against the demon which seeks to seduce her soul."

"A master stroke, Père Mourier! I could not have thought of a better one myself. Well, then, let us go quickly and take our place without danger of discovery."

"There will be no need to worry about our presence in the closet," Père Mourier winked at his English colleague. "The good Victorine, whom I have known for many years, is a pious soul. Moreover, she is spited because the patron did not wed her instead of Laurette, and it is human nature that she will try vindictively to make certain that the girl, once having snared the prize of marriage, lives up to it most strictly!"

I took this for an invitation for myself as well, and hopped upon the broad black hat of Père Mourier, which protected his florid face from the hot sun.

When they arrived at the home of Monsieur Claude Villiers, Père Mourier had a whispered conversation with Victorine while Father Lawrence pretended not to listen. I, myself at my ease on Père Mourier's black hat, heard everything. The French holy man had, it seemed, consoled Victorine on many a previous occasion when her grief at having lost two husbands (one from death by natural causes, the other because the man had run away with a young serving wench) became too much for her to bear alone. Hence there was a sympathetic bond between them, and, out of memory of this, the patron's housekeeper agreed to say nothing to her master and to hide them both in the spacious closet of his bedchamber. The patron, she believed, would return by seven that evening, would dine, and then summon his tender young bride to bed. At the moment, she informed them, Laurette was napping in her own room.

So the two cassocked ecclesiastics then secreted themselves in the closet, while she brought them sausage, bread, cheese and a half-bottle of good Anjou wine to quell their hunger—though I might have told her that their real hunger was for the white, soft flesh of gentle Laurette. And when they had made their meal, they drowsed. But I remained vigilant, for I wished to learn what mischief they intended the lovely virgin.

Sure enough, as Victorine had predicted, the senile old fool came back to the house shortly after the grandfather's clock in the hallway had struck seven, and, after performing his ablutions and changing his earth-stained garments, seated himself at the table and dined. Victorine informed him that the charming Laurette was feeling out of sorts, had napped much of the afternoon, and begged his indulgence to permit her to take her evening repast in her own chamber. "So be it," he snapped, "but you will tell M'lady Villiers that she is to attend me in my bedchamber directly after I have finished. If she demurs, remind her that she is my wife and that I have the right to thrash her with a switch if she does not obey in all things!"

Smirking at his own self-importance and the feeling of power it had given him to have such an autocratic order transmitted by the woman who had been his mistress to her far younger, more beautiful rival who was now his wife, scrawny old Claude Villiers ate a hearty supper, fortified by several glasses of Burgundy, and with his coffee had two glasses of cognac and then a cheroot. Finally, about eight-thirty, he got up rather unsteadily from the table and made his way to his bedchamber, his ugly features flushed and contorted with inflamed desire. He meant, this night, once and for all, to make Laurette his.

Victorine, out of compassion for the tender young damsel, had gone to Laurette's room to urge her to hasten to the master's bedchamber so as to avoid his wrath, and Laurette was consequently awaiting her elderly husband, seated in a chair, hands folded and eyes downcast. Monsieur Claude Villiers cackled with anticipatory glee at the sight of this demure, golden-haired virgin so docilely attendant on his bidding. With a loud belch, he ordered, "It is well for you, my pigeon, that you came to my summons. And now, without more ado, I bid you undress as I mean to consummate our marriage and rend that chaste barrier which turns you from innocent damsel to loving, obedient wife!"

Laurette by now had understood that any pleas to spare her modesty were little more than wasted breath, and so, rising from the chair, her milky cheeks red with shame, silently divested herself of her garments till she was deliciously nude from head to toe. Godiva's hair was a long and true shield to the prying eyes as she rode through Coventry, but Laurette could hide none of her beauties, for her two long, golden braids were at best decorative. Yet they gave her a look of exquisite girlishness and naiveté which, understandably, inflamed the already furious passions of this niggardly old fool.

"Now you will undress me, wife," the patron commanded. And when shy, tender Laurette hesitated, he snarled, "It will be a proof of your sweet docility as my wife, a sign that you accept your status. Otherwise, I shall thrash you till the blood flows and do so daily till you are my willing slave! Now do it quickly!"

Once again, with that enchanting intuition which seems to come to the aid of females in moments of crisis, Laurette submitted. Eyes downcast, cheeks aflame, she applied her trembling fingers to his garments till at last he appeared wisened, emaciated, hairy and naked before her, the obscene little dangler between his lean thighs flaunted to her chaste modesty. But to his delighted surprise, gentle Laurette, far from shrinking away at the manifestation of his maleness, hesitantly put out a little white hand and timidly took hold of the head of his cock.

"My little darling!" the overjoyed old patron cried in his reedy voice. "I have been too harsh with you I see, menacing you with beatings. I should have understood that, pure and innocent as you are, you needed time to comprehend the pleasures of the bed. Ah, Laurette, you do not know how happy you have made me now, nor how happy you shall soon make me. That's it, hold and fondle my cock and make it strong and powerful for the sweet ordeal of fitting it into that plump, hairy little slit between your round, white thighs!"

Laurette, though her blushes had spread nearly to her luscious white bubbies, continued to hold the head of her old husband's cock and now put her left arm round his waist, her eyes closed, and voluptuous shivers stealing through her divine nakedness. Now her thumb and forefinger took hold of the half-roused gnarled shaft and gave it a tender little pinch. "Oh, my beloved wife," he groaned, "how you entrance me! But come, let us take our pleasure on the soft broad bed, rather than tire ourselves by standing thus!"

In the closet, where the priests had kept their vigil for just such a sight as they now beheld, Père Mourier nudged his English confrère and whispered, "Mon dieu, does not the vision of such white, radiant naked flesh send flames of inspiration through your being?"

"Of a certainty, Père Mourier. It is, alas, risible to see that meager old man attempt to give so voluptuous and young a wench the pleasuring which only a robust and virile lover can afford her. And she is well made to accept such devotion, mark you. Ah, what finely rounded thighs, what delicious haunches! And that soft, sweetly dimpled belly, made to cushion a man's weight as he lies upon it, his firm member thrust to its very length deep within that sweet little golden downed nest of hers!" rhapsodized the English ecclesiastic.

"You are a man with spiritual kinship to me," said the fat French churchman. "I too share your desire for the charming Laurette. The two of us might contrive a way to educate her in her conjugal duties without robbing the worthy patron of his due. Yet perhaps I offend your moral scruples by intimating such a devious act?"

"Not so, not so in the least," declared the bluff English holy man, "my blood boils at the way her little white hand timidly acquaints itself with his dwarfed old garden tool. I would willingly spade her garden and harvest all the sweet bounty therein!"

"Methinks that if what we are watching now does not produce the consummation which will sanctify this union, we may achieve our desire," Père Mourier boldly declared. "For she is so young and impressionable and most devout. To thunder forth our wrath against her shirking her marital obligations will bring the naughty child to terms, mark my words upon it, Father Lawrence! But watch how she does her sweet maidenly best to bring M'sieu Villiers to point!"

Laurette had released her old husband's prick and permitted him to grasp her by the wrist and draw her, feverishly and pantingly, towards the connubial bed. The sweet girl stretched out upon it, hiding her face in the crook of one beautifully rounded white arm, while the patron, gasping and groaning like a fish out of water, scrambled onto the bed and knelt beside his adorable young bride. "Oh, I implore you, my little pigeon, to go on with what you were just doing," he whined in his cackling voice. "I must possess you or die of frustration! Take hold of my prick again, my sweetling, and nestle it in the soft warm cove of your little hand, that it may grow to requisite vigor!"

Laurette dutifully lifted her other hand and groped for his still-dormant weapon. Her fingertips tickled and glided over it from head to balls, while the two eavesdropping clergymen held their breath and stared through the crack in the closet door at what was taking place.

Gradually, under her delicious ministrations, his cock hardened to commendable size and length, though it could in no way compare with the potency of Pierre Larrieu, and still less with the mighty ramrods possessed by those two who espied this intimate scene from their closet hiding place. Meanwhile, the patron, his face screwed up in a rictus of tortured bliss, scrambled with his bony fingers over Laurette's upper thighs, her dimpled belly, and her golden ringlets which covered her soft, pink-lipped cunny.

"Oh, enough, my beauty," he groaned at last, "you will make me lose it all, and I must put it deep into your little slit! Open your legs, my pigeon, and prepare yourself for my charge! I will make you beg for mercy, as I promised!"

He crouched now between her obediently spread thighs, and with his trembling fingers sought to wrench apart the sweet warm corals of her quim so that he might engage his tool within that amorous antechamber. But no sooner had he fitted the nozzle of his organ between those soft pouting prisms, then his body stiffened and his eyes bulged glassily and he uttered a raucous cry: "Ohhh, I cannot hold it back, oh, you have undone me with your sorcery, you little vixen!"

And sure enough, there dribbled from his needle a few gouts of sticky essence, but they were not lodged within the matrix that he had so boastfully sworn to fill. Recovering at length from the seizure, he at last procured a cambric kerchief and mopped her thighs and belly and his own once-again dwindled tool. Then, still resolute despite his failures, he had recourse to a bottle of brandy which he had caused Victorine to place on a little table near the bed for just such an occasion. He gulped down half a glass and then sputtering, and with tears in his eyes, declared that he had hardly begun the battle for her maidenhead, which would fall like the very walls of Jericho before the moon set in the heavens.

During this scene, Père Mourier and Father Lawrence heatedly expatiated on the young, voluptuous beauties of Laurette's lovely naked body. The French ecclesiastic held for her bubbies, whose impudent, jouncy globes entranced him most of all, whereas the virile English churchman fancied the plump rounders of her backside and the appetizing golden-fleeced mound of her Venus.

"But my dear confrère," Père Mourier concluded, "there is really no need to apportion out all these delicacies, since the two of us shall share and share alike once the sweet and timid maiden comes under our sway."

"But how can you be certain that she will?" Father Lawrence demanded.

"You are forgetting Victorine owes me many favors. And, in return, she has promised not only to secrete us in this fine closet and to bring us wine and food to enliven our long wait, but also, after the worthy patron starts to snore, to bring his gentle bride a message from her rascally lover. She will flee to him, and it is then that we shall apprehend her in the very act of wishing to go forth to an adulterous tryst. Then we shall have her, I warrant you. But, watch now, the brandy has given him false courage and he will try again!"

It was quite true. As Laurette lay submissively on her back, her face still hidden by her covering arm, the scrawny patron had returned to bed. Now he was fiddling with his own diminished tool, panting and cackling like a madman loose in Bedlam as he sought to rigidify himself to adequacy for the delicious task. But for him, alas, it was to prove more arduous than any of the labors of Hercules—and I do not refer to the thus-named overseer who, I do not doubt in the last, could have indeed broken through Laurette's maidenhead with a single stab of his sexual weapon.

Finally, confessing himself defeated, he piteously begged her to grant him once again the touch of her little hand upon his private parts. She did so resignedly, uttering a desolate little sigh. He knelt beside her, his eyes closed, his head thrown back, surrendering himself entirely to her ministrations. Her soft white little fingers enlaced themselves around his drooping shaft, then fondled and tickled his balls, then returned to stroking and daintily pinching the head of his useless protuberance. Finally, with a groan, he crawled between her thighs and flung himself down atop her. His hands clutched her white, swelling bubbies with a desperate urgency as he ground his loins against her sweet mount. But, try as he would, even the sight and the feel of her naked body against his did not have the needful effect. Finally, with a long, heart-rending groan that almost made the two hiding priests chuckle—so dolorous was its lamentation and renunciation—Monsieur Villiers kissed Laurette chastely on the brow and stretched out on his back beside her. In a moment or two he was fast asleep. His fatigue, as well as the brandy, had withdrawn him from the tourney this night.

"Now it will be but a few moments till Victorine brings in the spurious message," Père Mourier whispered excitedly.

It was, in all, a quarter of an hour before the door gently opened and Victorine stuck her head inside. Hearing the snores of her master, she took heart, opened the door a little more and tiptoed towards the great bed. She put her hand out to touch Laurette's naked breast. The young virgin, not yet fallen asleep, was about to start up with a cry when Victorine laid a finger across her lips, murmuring, "Shhhh! Do not wake the master, my little one. I have a message for you from Pierre Larrieu!"

"Oh, Victorine, what is it? Oh, how I've longed to hear from my sweetheart. I thought he had forsaken me and left the village."

"No, my gentle lamb, not so. He has told me to come to you and bid you meet him out on that same grassy knoll where you last had a rendezvous with him. Come, I will take you to your chamber and there you can dress and hasten to your lover."

Laurette carefully crept out of bed, a naked young goddess, and followed Victorine back to her own chamber. The two priests rose, stretching their limbs and suppressing their gasps as the circulation was restored to their bodies. In a trice, they were alert and eager for what would follow. "We shall give the naughty little wench a moment or two to clothe herself, and then we shall go into her chamber and sermonize her," Père Mourier decreed.

They gave her all of three minutes before they left the patron's bedroom and went to Laurette's door. Père Mourier knocked twice, very softly. Laurette, doubtless supposing it was Victorine, hastened to open the door, and then recoiled with a stifled little cry of terror. What a bewitching picture she made, for she was clad only in her drawers and camisole. She had doused her lovely face with cold water to remove the trace of tears she had shed at the repugnance of this last interlude with her distasteful husband. And she was ravishingly desirable, those two long, golden braids hanging down to her waist, her round bubbies tumultuously heaving in her apprehension at beholding her Father confessor and his English colleague.

"What—what are you doing here, mon père?" she gasped as Father Lawrence deftly closed the door behind him and drew the bolt.

Père Mourier shook a fat, admonishing finger at her. "Oh, my poor child, I have come in the nick of time to dissuade you from committing the most adulterous wickedness.

"And now you commit another sin, that of lying to your good Father confessor," the obese holy man rebuked her in a pompous voice. "I had asked good Father Lawrence to come with me on making my rounds of the parish this evening, and, when we called here, the good Victorine had just received a message from a little boy whom this vaurien, Pierre Larrieu, had sent with this infamous summons. Thank heaven she had the presence of mind and the loyalty to her dear master to inform me of this message, or even now you might be in that wretch's arms for a sinful rendezvous. Oh, my daughter, you have put your feet upon the pathway to perdition. And look—you bedeck yourself in your flimsiest undergarments to entice this forbidden lover to the body which belongs solely to the worthy Claude Villiers."

"Oh, mon père, I cannot help it," Laurette sobbed. "If you only knew how horrible it is for me to have to lie abed with that vile old man! It is true that my Pierre is a bastard and so cannot wed me, yet I would rather be his harlot and lie with him in the fields than suffer the indignities which M'sieu Villiers subjects me to in the guise of wedlock. What am I to do, mon père?"

And with this, the lovely girl flung herself down on her knees and clasped her hands and held them up to the obese French holy man, as the tears ran down her flushed cheeks.

"I will tell you this, my daughter," thundered Père Mourier, "if you visit that roué, I will surely excommunicate you! I intend to tell the patron how you are ready to cuckold him only a few moments after he had sought with all his devotion and gentleness to possess you."

"Oh, oh, no, you would not tell him that! Oh, I would die of shame! And you must not curse my darling Pierre. He is honest and good and kind, and his only sin is loving me. Please, Père Mourier, forgive him, and forgive me too."

She looked up at him, her eyes blinded with tears, and she clasped his fat thighs with her beautiful arms in the most exquisite attitude of supplication. The voluptuous effect of such beauty in submission was instantly visible as Père Mourier's massive cock jabbed out of his cassock.

"There is perhaps a way, my daughter," he said hoarsely, with an imperceptible little glance at the smiling Father Lawrence, who stood behind the kneeling girl, "whereby you can make your penance and yet save your marriage, without committing this deadly sin with the young scoundrel."

"Tell me how, mon père! I will do anything you ask," Laurette avowed.

"Having made much study of the ebullient nature of male and female," the fat French priest sententiously began, "I think I can evaluate your case astutely, my poor benighted daughter. The holy estate of matrimony is surely to be sought for one of your lowly status, true enough. But in your particular instance, since I have seen with mine own eyes how lasciviously inclined your secret nature is—do not try to deny it, my child, for you recall that I beheld you and this Pierre Larrieu about to commit adultery once before—my belief is that, once you have overcome the silly vapours and timidities natural to your physical condition of virginity, you will no longer dread the legal contact with your illustrious husband. Therefore, once we remove these vapours and these timidities, my dear child, you will be amazed at how little inclination you will have to seeking out this young wretch for your illicit pleasures, because you will be edified sufficiently to partake of them naturally and honorably with your own husband. Tell me this quickly—has he yet taken your virginity?"

"Oh, no, no," Laurette gasped and hid her blushing tear-stained face in the folds of the fat priest's cassock.

"Then this verifies my supposition and my theory, my dear child," Père Mourier resumed. "Inwardly, your lascivious desires make you yearn for coition, while at the same moment your virginal hymen imposes upon you an abhorrence and frigidity which defeat your nature. If we effect to remove the latter, the former may be then fully channeled towards the greater pleasure of a lawful consort. And thereby lies the penance which I shall set you here and now, my sweet Laurette."

She looked up at him wide-eyed, not quite understanding his sly and cunning aim. "Wh-what must I do, then, mon père?"

"Prepare to yield your maidenhead to me, your Father confessor, who has known you since you were a tender child. I will thus be your devout initiator, my charming child, and educate you towards your proper conjugal duties."

"Oh! You—you cannot mean..." Laurette

stammered as she rose to her feet and shrank back, eyes huge with stupefaction.

"You misunderstand me, my daughter," Père Mourier suavely interposed. "I do not mean to take you in lust as would this unworthy Pierre. No, my daughter, it will be an act of edification, simply that and nothing more. And I absolve you from any sin, since I have prevented you from your commission of adultery this night. Is that not so, Father Lawrence?"

"He speaks the truth, Laurette," the English ecclesiastic corroborated his French colleague.

The lovely Laurette did not know what face to put upon this situation, as she still could not believe her ears. But the fat priest lost no time in acquainting her with his intention, since he at once doffed his hat and cassock and stood in all his hairy nakedness, his massive cock already savagely distended. "Nature has better endowed me, my child, than even your forbidden lover," he declared. "Now to begin your penance, remove the camisole and drawers and place yourself in repose upon your bed. I will attend you, and zealously seek to instruct you in these duties in which you have been so remiss with your loyal, loving husband."

"Oh, mon père, you aren't going to—oh, surely, you don't mean to do this to me?" Laurette gasped incredulously.

"It is up to you, my child. If you will persist in shirking your obligations, and if you are still drawn towards this adulterous rogue, then he will be excommunicated, and your husband shall be told why. Moreover, because of your wicked obstinacy, I shall regrettably be compelled to scourge you to chasten your wicked spirit and suppress you heinous nature. You have your choice, Laurette."

"Oh, I would die before I let you hurt my poor Pierre, and I could not bear to have the patron know my loathing of him." Laurette wrung her hands in her dilemma. "But at least, to spare me greater shame, do ask Father Lawrence not to witness what you intend to do."

"But he is here, my daughter, exactly to insure to you that mine is not an act of lust, but only that of simple instruction," the fat priest slyly responded.

Seeing that she was well trapped, judging that the sacrifice of her maidenhead to her own Father confessor would be less onerous for her and Pierre than the alternative, Laurette, softly weeping, hesitantly removed her camisole and then at last tugged down her drawers and stepped out of them. Both priests uttered gasps of admiration at the gleaming white, naked statuary of her suple young body. Her instinctive maidenly modesty still strong, Laurette clapped both hands to her cunny and bowed her head.

"You have done well, my daughter," Père Mourier declared, his voice thick with impatient passion, "and this shows good faith. Now accede to my other order, which is to lay yourself down upon your bed and make ready for me, your sanctified initiator."

Laurette reluctantly obeyed. Upon her back, a hand over her eyes, her other little hand clutched into a tight fist at one naked luscious haunch, she awaited her perilous moment. His eyes gleaming with avaricious concupiscence, the fat, hairy churchman clambered onto the bed and knelt beside the shivering, naked penitent. His fat, hairy hands roamed leisurely over her smooth belly, her panting teats, and the valley between them, her tender sides, the slopes of her delicious hips. I knew I could not save Laurette from both these lusty suitors, and I confess I was impelled by curiosity to witness precisely how the tender maiden would react when the destructive breach was made against her cherished virgin's seal. Perching on the other side of the pillow on which her golden head now reposed, I watched the French clergyman.

For all his greedy desire, he did not hasten, for which I gave him credit. His hands caressed the shivering thighs and flanks and belly and breasts of the naked virgin, till he was shivering too. She kept her arm tightly thrust over her lovely blue eyes to hide the sight, and I will grant that, if Claude Villiers was unappetizing, Père Mourier could not be considered a tastier bridegroom, save only in one respect: his throbbing, swollen cock. And yet, since it was by this sole part of his anatomy that Laurette was to be "edified," it did not really matter that he was hairy, fat, and ugly of visage.

Gently he made Laurette part her thighs, and while his fat right hand smoothed and stroked her inner thigh, his left forefinger very delicately tangled amid the golden love-curls of her silt and tickled the plump corals of her cunny. Her body was tense and quivering in an attitude of defense, yet when his fingertip at last brushed the soft hidden labia of her virgin cunt, she uttered a tremulous little gasp, and unconsciously arched up her loins and belly as if eager to taste more of this exquisite friction. Père Mourier shot a triumphant glance at Father Lawrence as if to say, "Did I not tell you she had a lascivious nature?" and accelerated his tickling. The pad of his forefinger now began to rub in a slow circular movement 'round and 'round the dainty little cleft. Presently the golden love-curls seemed to become ruffled, and there peeped through the sweet pink petals of that flower, which Monsieur Claude Villiers had had longer to pluck and was still far from plucking, a little nub of virgin flesh. Laurette's naked breasts began to rise and fall with a spasmodic rhythm now, and her head turned restlessly from side to side, though she still hid her eyes from the florid, passion-contracted visage of her Father confessor.

"Do I hurt you thus far, my daughter?" he unctuously queried.

"N—no, mon—mon père," Laurette quavered. Long rippling tremors now beset her rounded white thighs, traversing from the knees on along into her gaping crotch and I perceived that the rosy buds of her nipples had stiffened, and now projected out in taut, crisp firmness, a symbol of her wakening to the first true carnal evocation of all her womanly senses.

"You see, my child, how little there is to fear?" he told her, as his finger now moved to find the nodule of her virgin clitoris. Having come upon it, he delicately worked it back and forth, till Laurette wriggled and convulsively squirmed her hips this way and that, little inarticulate sighs and gasps coming from her parted lips. Her toes twisted and flexed and the muscles of her lovely white calves shuddered as the amorous excitement began to seethe through every nerve and sinew of her luscious body.

By this time, I could see the enchanting pink crevice formed by the two dainty, plump, parted lips, like a flower opening its petals to the sun. His titillations had found the key to Laurette's strongbox of desire, and the suspicious moisture about those adorable labia proved that the astute science of this licentious holy man had rendered the tender virgin far more willing and ready than even Pierre Larrieu had been able to do out there on the grassy knoll.

"Oh, what a delicious, pink, sweet soft cunt!" he breathed in rapturous admiration. "See, Father Lawrence, how it longs to be liberated of that obstreperous barrier which alone denies our sweet Laurette the boon of marital consummation! Courage, my daughter, the moment is not far off when the veil of mystery shall be lifted from your sweet blue eyes and you shall behold the glory of fleshly union. And imbued with this newly acquired fervor which I shall teach you, you can then welcome your worthy husband to your bed with eager arms and readied thighs!"

Now with his thumbs and forefingers, Père Mourier pinched apart the sweet, pink lips of Laurette's maiden grotto, and, bowing his head, applied a loud and smacking kiss upon her very core. She arched herself, deliciously and wantonly, though I am certain it was done out of her subconscious nature, just as the good father had predicted. Now I heard the sloshing of his tongue as he darted it deep within her chalice, and Laurette uttered a shrill cry nigh unto ecstasy as she dug her hands into the sheets of her bed, her widely opened eyes staring down at him, her nostrils dilating and shrinking tempestuously.

"Oh, mon père, what are you doing to me! Oh, oh, I can't bear it, I shall faint, you are driving me wild, mon père!" she babbled.

"Yes, my daughter, now you are ready for your initiation. I feel your sweet little clit throbbing like an engine just inside the soft mouth of your virgin cunny," Père Mourier tersely exclaimed. "Your belly quivers and jerks, and your skin is warm and moist with longing. Prepare yourself, my daughter, for the moment of consummation."

With this, still keeping her lips well pried apart, he edged the taut head of his bludgeon just inside them and gave a little push to insure the proper position against the stubborn barrier. Laurette moaned, turned her face to one side and closed her eyes, but the heaving of her flinty-tipped bubbies and the spasmodic tensions which raced along her yawning thighs betrayed her mounting impatience to learn at last the way of a man with a maid.

He gave another thrust, and Laurette winced and uttered a shrill little cry, "Aahh, it hurts me, mon père!"

"That is the proof of your chastity, my daughter. Courage, now, for the hurt will soon be over then your state of consummation will bring you towards that bliss which you have so long sought."

Now, carefully letting himself down upon her, mashing her sweet, soft belly with his own fat paunch, his hands gliding under her backside to grip the plump satiny rounds and thus steer himself towards the achievement of her "edification," Père Mourier set his teeth and shoved forward with a mighty lunge. Laurette's body writhed and stiffened; her hands at once clenched into little fists that began to hammer at his naked back, and her knees rose up on either side of him, yawning hugely apart, then clashing together at him in the wildest protest. At the same time, a shrill squeal like that of a sacrificed animal burst from her throat, but the deed was done.

"Ah, I am in her to my balls, Father Lawrence!" Père Mourier exulted. "How tight the little darling is! I can feel the walls of her womb kiss and clutch my cock ever so lovingly. Oh, what delight, what rapture! Never in all my days have I fucked so sweet, so young, so tasty a morsel: Never before have I felt the grip of so tight a sheath as Laurette's!"

She had twisted her face to one side, and her fists still futilely beat against his massive, sweating back. But the harpoon had plunged to the depths within her, and she was pinioned by his weight and by his grip on her bottom cheeks. Well in her saddle, he now began to fuck her with slow but deep and eviscerating stabs of his massive weapon. The first few times, she sobbed and wriggled and cried out, "Aahh, arrr, oh, mon père, mon père, you are hurting me so!" But as he began to establish a smooth and mellifluous rhythm of back and forth and in and out, his massive ramrod drawing just to the lips of her distended crevice and then driving home till their hairs mingled,

Laurette began to moan and to arch herself to meet his delving digs.

Father Lawrence watched all this, though I do not think it was for scientific purposes, for the black silk stuff of his cassock thrust out at a prodigious angle at the point of his loins. At moments, Laurette's glazed, supremely dilated eyes rested on him, but unseeingly, for all her life now was concentrated into the tight, no-longer-virginal channel of her quaking cunt. Her fists no longer beat their supplicating tattoo upon her ravisher's back, but instead her fingers clawed at his shoulders like talons as she met his charges. Now her naked calves clamped 'round his hairy thighs as she locked herself to him and resigned herself to the new-found pleasure. The forfeiture of her maidenhead was truly only the first step towards the voluptuousness which her "instruction" was meant to achieve.

"How she claws at me and clutches me, this darling vixen," Père Mourier hoarsely declared to his watching colleague. "Oh, how gloriously tight she is, even though I have pronged and stretched her quim with all my vigor! Each time I draw my cock back, I feel the narrow walls of her cunny clench and grip after me, as if begging me to return—there, Laurette, my passionate daughter, and there, and there too—do you feel me in your cunt, does my cock make you know what it is to be a woman at last, my daughter?"

"Aahhrr, oh, yes, yes, mon père," Laurette moaned in her delirium, rolling her head from side to side, taking tighter hold of her ravisher's shoulders, and reaching up to clutch her beautiful thighs around his fat, hairy bottom, "Do not spare me, let me make a good penance, mon père! Oh, I am fainting from your thrusts, you stretch and gouge me there, oh, mon père, hurry, hurry!"

"In a moment, my daughter, I will lave your hurts

with good hot spunk! It is an infallible antidote for the lacerations of a maiden's hymen as you found it once a boon for your scored bottom. Hold tight to me, my daughter, and strive with me mightily for the redemption of your womanly estate!" he panted. His fingers gouged her quaking bottom cheeks, and now he began to quicken his strokes within her deeply harpooned cunny, making Laurette gasp and jerk each time the hilt of his prong sheathed in her clinging, tight scabbard. Now her head had fallen back, her eyes rolling to the whites, and her nostrils opening and closing incessantly. Her teeth chattered, and her red lips were moist and parted and trembling. A tumult raged within her loins, and now the moment had come to slake it. Drawing a deep breath, Père Mourier flung himself once more to the charge, his hairs grinding against Laurette's golden cunny curls. Then his body shook and vibrated as he reached his climax. Laurette uttered a raucous cry as she felt the hot deluge gush along her distended love canal. Yet he had not brought her to climax, for I have observed that a virgin rarely achieves her paroxysm after an initial pronging, since not only the twinges of her shattered maidenhead but also the long enforced continence which her parents had imposed upon her most naturally prevent her ardent temperament from erotic expansion in this wise.

He withdrew his bloody blade, and Father Lawrence solicitously handed him a cloth whereby to wipe away the irrefutable evidence of Laurette's chastity. The English ecclesiastic had procured a ewer of water, and now dampened another cloth and sponged Laurette's sweating forehead and cheeks, the while avidly staring at her sprawled nakedness.

"Is—is my penance over now?" Laurette murmured faintly. Her knees were still arched but had come together; her bubbies still rose and fell with erotic fervor. Père Mourier uttered a sigh of satiation. "I shall ask my colleague to pronounce the last portion of your penance, my child," he said as he seated himself on a chair and, taking another of the dampened cloths, mopped his own perspiring brow and chest with it.

"Oh, do so, I implore you, mon père," Laurette breathed, letting her legs down and unconsciously spreading them so that once again the access to her sweetest treasure was exposed to the gleaming eyes of the English ecclesiastic. "I have never felt such sensations, I shall swoon, I know I shall, and yet there is still torment within me."

"Then it is I who shall help you overcome that torment, my child," Father Lawrence stoutly declared as he drew off his cassock and joined her, virile and naked and sinewy, upon the rumpled bed. Turning her gently onto her side to face him, he kissed her lips tenderly, while his left hand stroked her quivering bare bottom. Laurette uttered a little sigh and closed her eyes and shivered, but did not draw away from him. Yet when his massive cock prodded against her tender belly she gasped and glanced down, then blushingly whispered, "Oh, tell me that is not part of my penance too, Your Reverence? It will surely never go inside me now!"

"But quite the contrary, my daughter, since my confrère has already prepared the terrain so well, you will see how you accommodate yourself to its dimensions. Now clasp me tightly with your white arms and kiss me soundly, while we say our prayers together to make you a good and loving wife!"

Laurette shiveringly and trustingly complied, and Father Lawrence began to cup and squeeze her bubbies with his right hand, while he slyly rubbed the tip of his massive cock along her abdomen and thence to the furry niche of her just deflowered cunny. She wriggled and squirmed against him, her arms tightly locked around his shoulders, giving him back kiss for affectionate kiss, but keeping her eyes modestly closed as befitted so gentle a maiden newly come upon her wifely state.

"I would not compel you against your will, my daughter," he said gently. "So, with your little hand, you must yourself guide this eager pilgrim into your soft bower. You shall yourself prescribe the extent to which it shall go wandering!'

Lulled by his kindly guidance, and her senses already inflamed by the good work of her initiator, Père Mourier, Laurette shyly took hold of the good father's massive cockhead. Tentatively, she rubbed it very lightly against the gaping pink lips of her love-slit, gasping and wincing at the faint twinges which recalled to her the taking of her chastity. Meanwhile, his left hand roved all over her bottom, and finally a forefinger slid down the sinuous, ambery cleft which separated those succulent hemispheres till he found the dainty, crinkly fissure of her anus. He began to prod the lips very lightly, and Laurette moaned with sexual fever as this caress wakened all her innately libidinous tendencies. At last, with a gasp, she fitted the head of his cock between her soft cunny lips, and then frantically locked her arms about his shoulders and clung to him in trusting confidence that he would do the rest.

Slowly, Father Lawrence edged his blade along the pathway already hollowed out for him by his French colleague. Laurette caught her breath as she felt his turgid ramrod sink along the quivering interior of her love-channel. Her right thigh rose to clamp over his leg as she arched herself to him. At the same moment, his fingertip prodded inside the clenching lips of her bumhole; thus impelled, Laurette glued her mouth to his, and, her naked bubbies flattening to his surging chest, totally surrendered herself. With a single massive thrust, he dug inside her to his balls, silencing her long-drawn moan of ecstasy with a furiously impassioned kiss.

Then he began to fuck the beautiful, golden-haired maiden—or, more strictly speaking, young bride—and Laurette feverishly responded. Père Mourier looked on with jaundiced eye. He could perhaps content himself with the thought he had awakened all the exquisite response, but, alas, his confrère would profit therefrom. Still, he managed a smile of consolation at the notion that there would be other penances and other expiations whereby once again he could savoringly enjoy the golden-haired, white-skinned loveliness of this naked beauty.

Now Father Lawrence slid his right forefinger down between their bodies and attacked her already turgid clitoris. Artfully he rubbed and rolled the little button, whilst his other forefinger foraged slowly and deeply inside her bottomhole. Synchronizing this dual manipulation with his own regular digs and withdrawals, he soon brought Laurette to moaning ecstasy, and at last, digging her fingernails into his sides, she threw back her head and cried out in wordless rapture as she felt his violent gush inundate her. And, by the quaking of her own appeased, naked body against his, she let flow her own secret tides to meet his own, and thus attained her first womanly climax.

CHAPTER THIRTEEN

If tender Laurette had procured a pardon for Pierre Larrieu and at the same time a remission of her failure to show herself to be a proper dutiful wife by the simple expedient of surrendering her maidenhead to Père Mourier (with Father Lawrence making doubly sure it could no longer existed), she also managed to learn a good deal about her own disposition. It was, quite simply, that the removal of her hymen had, at one fell swoop, whisked away all her virginal vapors—oddly enough, just as fat Père Mourier had predicted—and she found could give herself up with willing heart and eager cunt to carnal pleasuring.

I learned as much when the good Victorine attended her in her own chamber the very next day after this memorable hymeneal martyrdom to which she had been subjected. Laurette, before her mirror, clad in only camisole and drawers, had decided to undo her long, thick plaits and comb out her beautiful golden tresses to form a cascade which would be more feminine and womanly. For, after all, she was now truly a woman, having, in the short time it took Père Mourier to pierce her maiden seal, achieved that miraculous transition.

"May I aid Madame in combing out her hair?" Victorine offered.

"No, many thanks, dear Victorine," the golden-haired bride cheerfully replied. "But you would be doing me a great service if you would tell me truly whether you received a message last night from my sweetheart, Pierre Larrieu."

Victorine flushed and she looked down rather guiltily. "But of a certainty, did I not come to the patron's bedchamber to deliver such a message?" she managed.

Laurette turned to her with a sweet smile and put her hand over the housekeeper's. "Yes, in truth you did, but could it not have been a false message? Be honest with me, Victorine, and I shall be your loyal friend and aide in this household. I will have my husband increase your wages and do all that which will please you. For, to be equally honest with you, I love my Pierre and I shall never love the master whom you wished yourself to wed."

Victorine hesitated, for to incur the wrath of the Father confessor of the village was not a prospect she relished. But Laurette, again with marvelous intuition, read in the housekeeper's face the struggle, and she promptly laid that fear to rest. "Look you, Victorine, I will give you my word of honor not to betray you to Père Mourier, whom I suspect of having arranged to send you to me with such a message so that I would hurry to my lover and fall into the lewd clutches of that cunning churchman. And, more, I will leave the field open to you with my husband, for, if I ever have the opportunity, I mean to leave him and run away with my true lover. I am not and never will be your rival, dear Victorine. What say you?"

"You—you—then you are not angry with me? I could not help it, he made me do it, Madame," Victorine blubbered.

"Oh, no," Laurette smiled. "I have done a good deal of thinking since last night, and in a way Père Mourier has done me a better service than he guessed. For now that I am no longer a maiden but I am still under my husband's protection. And if I have a rendezvous with my lover and am gotten with child by him, no one can dare say that it is not the patron's doing, for I shall faithfully and humbly perform my duties with M'sieu Villiers. So that is understood—and now will you be my ally?"

"Gladly, Madame," Victorine sighed.

"Then take this little ring with a seed pearl as a present from me. It was given me by my husband but he will not miss it and by rights it should have gone to you anyway. In return, I want you to get a message to Pierre from me—and this a true one, mind you!—that I am longing to see him when it can be arranged discreetly."

"I swear I will do it Madame, and I will not betray you to Père Mourier."

"Thank you, my dear Victorine. And now go prepare breakfast and I shall wake my husband. I must be attentive to him so he will never suspect where my heart belongs."

How truly the charming girl had matured in a single night! Perhaps all would yet be well with this tender damsel. Yet the presence of Père Mourier and Father Lawrence and their combined influence with her senile fool of a husband was not the best augur for the future. I told myself I would pay close attention to their machinations against her and aid her cause whenever I could do so.

But fate was to intervene in quite an unexpected way on behalf of Laurette. For exactly two days after she had held secret counsel with good Dame Victorine, news came from the hamlet of Fontbleu, a hundred miles to the south of Languecuisse, that the worthy Monsieur Gilles Henriot and his good dame, Agnes, had died suddenly of the flux, leaving their little daughter, Marisia, who was still in the spring of her youth, an orphan. Learning this news, Claude

Villiers mourned deeply, for Agnes was his younger sister. He thereupon sent word by the horseman who had ridden to him with the gloomy tidings that Marisia was to be sent here to him post haste so that he might become her guardian and she the sweet niece of his young bride, Laurette.

A day later, Marisia arrived in the company of the old fat steward to Gilles Henriot, and was given into the keeping of her elderly uncle. She was an entrancing little beauty. Black hair, glossy as a raven's wing, fell in a thick sheaf past her shoulders. Her face was oval and saucy with full red lips, gray-green eyes narrowly spaced by the bridge of a dainty snub nose whose thin, glaring wings bespoke a merciful and warm-blooded nature, and high-set, slanting cheeks of an ivory complexion that was bewitching. Yet her figure was even more fetching. She was nearly as tall as Laurette herself, and Marisia possessed a superbly developed, already bold pair of pear-shaped bubbies set closely together and whose crests pushed insolently at the bodice of her thin blouse. Supple of waist, she owned lithe, sleek haunches and an impudently jutting pair of oval-contoured bottom cheeks set above her willowy long, gracefully slim thighs and entrancingly sinuous calves.

The old vintner was much overjoyed at the affectionate welcome given by his young bride to his niece, and beamed fatuously as he saw the two embrace. Yes, he thought to himself, in his declining years, Dame Fortune had smiled upon him and given him a bride who, though at the outset repugnant and averse to his affections, had miraculously learned her place and would warm his sheets as zestfully as a harlot from the streets. And, it must be admitted also, his eyes dwelt reflectively on the budding charms of his tender young niece.

Marisia was installed in a chamber next to

Laurette's own, and that afternoon the two young beauties closeted themselves to become better acquainted.

"I will do my best to make you happy in this, your new home, dear Marisia," Laurette tenderly told her charming niece, "and we shall be fast friends, for you are not too many years behind my own age, and I have need of friends."

Marisia giggled roguishly, forward minx that she was. Her voice was rich and husky, like a coquette's: "This I doubt not, knowing my uncle well from what my poor parents have often told me of him."

"Hush, dear Marisia, you must not show any resentment. I have learned that lesson myself at great cost. It is best to humor him and pretend to be fond of him."

"To be sure, so that you can go unsuspected to your lover, dear Aunt Laurette," was the tender girl's amazing response.

"Marisia! How can you speak of such a thing! You are much too young to know about love."

"Not so, Aunt Laurette. I, too, am sorrowful to have left my home, for there was a boy named Everard, who did kiss and fondle me till my senses were all awhirl. Is your lover very handsome, my dear Aunt Laurette? Everard is fair and tall, with the deepest blue eyes," the little hoyden sighed.

"Oh!" Laurette blushed. "M-mine is blond and tall, too, and gentle and kind."

"All of which Uncle Claude is not. I have heard my poor Maman say that one day he would come to his death from tumbling wenches. He has, you know, a heart that is none too sound. Maman said she did not know how it chanced that he was not taken with a stroke when coupling with some wench who struck his fancy."

"Marisia, you must not speak of such vulgar

things! You are still a child, and—"

"Pooh," retorted the bold hoyden, making an impudent face, "I have almost coupled myself, Aunt Laurette, or next best to it. For my Everard, not wanting to get me big me with child, did use his tongue and finger instead of his big prick in my little slit!"

"Ohhh!" was all the scarlet-faced Laurette could say at this incredible declaration. Yet what the minx had just revealed to her had planted a seed of fantasy in her brain; if that was true, then, by coddling and cozening the old patron in the course of showing him her willingness to perform her conjugal duties, she might well excite him beyond measure. And if he were then carried off by a seizure as punishment for his lecherous overindulgence, then she would be widowed and free to marry whomsoever she pleased. Nay, more—she would fall heir to his estate and all his gold.

Cautiously, still overwhelmed by the fanciful prospect which Marisia's bold candor had evoked, she hazarded: "My sweet niece, would it please you to see your Everard again?"

"Oh, Aunt Laurette, it would be such heaven," Marisia eagerly avowed, clapping her soft ivory hands together in glee. "But how can it be? He is the son of my parents' steward, and must live with his father to look after the house and lands."

"Well, then, if we are very nice to your Uncle Claude," the beauty wheedled, "we might crave the boon from him of letting Everard come to visit here for a fortnight."

"How I love you, Aunt Laurette!" Marisia flung her slim arms 'round her young aunt's neck and kissed her fiercely. "Oh, I will do anything you tell me, that Uncle Claude may grant such a boon."

Another idea had come to Laurette, experienced woman that she had become by the miracle of her loss of virginity; she had remembered the covetous glow in her elderly husband's eyes when they had fallen on Marisia. "I think I may know a way, my sweetling," she murmured, "but it may not be to your taste."

"But tell me, dear Tante Laurette!"

"I have swiftly learned that, by humoring your uncle in bed, he is of better spirits and more likely to grant a favor. No—no, I should not even think of such an odious thing, you are but a child...."

"I am not a child, Tante Laurette," Marisia impertinently declared with a toss of her raven head. "I warrant I know almost as much about fucking as you do!"

"Ohh, Marisia, such talk is scandalous!" Laurette was blushing with confusion.

"But I do, dear Tante! At our farm, I saw the dogs and pigs coupling, and the bull with the cow, and Everard told me how it was done 'twixt man and maid. It was only fear of getting me big with child that kept him from putting his big prick into me—though once I let him rub the head just over my little crack! And I often played with it, making it jet its thick cream over my hand."

"I cannot believe what I hear, my darling niece—you, so young, to speak of hand-fucking!" Laurette breathed. But the ingenious plan whereby she might win her Pierre was already fomenting behind that pure brow of hers. I perched atop her golden head, and, though I could of course not divine what was passing inside, I followed her drift fairly well.

"Pooh," said Marisia, tossing her lovely head till her raven curls danced. "You cannot know much more, being only wed a few short weeks to my old fool of an uncle!"

At this, Laurette's white cheeks were dyed a furious carmine. "However, I may dare suggest a way to win your Everard's presence here on holiday—but I will not countenance it unless you swear to me you will not sin so greatly that you will bear a child."

"I know many ways of pleasing Everard without fucking, dear Tante Laurette," was Marisia's impudent boast. "There is the way of tickling with one's hand or finger, also with one's tongue—"

"Stop, I cannot bear to have you speak so boldly of such things done best under the sheets with the candles blown out," gasped the beautiful Laurette.

"Then I will show you what I mean, dear Tante!"

"With your uncle?" Laurette hazarded. Ah, what a shrewd and sweet minx she had become! For assuredly, let both beauties enter his bedchamber to do his carnal homage, and even the heart of a wholesome, sanguine rogue would bound affrightedly; old Claude Villiers would surely be carried off by a seizure the like of which two such entrancing conspiratresses could procure with the vision of their naked forms!

"If it would please you," was Marisia's artful reply.

"Not me, you saucy wench, but your uncle. And he would be so enraptured, I warrant, as to grant you any boon you sought!"

"Then it is as good as done," Marisia boldly giggled.

"So be it," said Laurette, blushing again. "Tonight, I shall bring you into our conjugal chamber. I shall keep watch that he does you no great harm."

"Bah, he cannot! My poor papa said, once in my hearing, that Uncle Claude was all talk and no prick!" Marisia avowed. And so the exquisite plot was sworn to!

And so that night, when, in better humor than he had been since his wedding night, the old patron entered his bedchamber, he found his golden-haired bride reclining on the bed in a thin white shift that modestly veiled her charms to her ankles. Yet she smiled on him and sweetly held out her arms to him, saying, "M'sieu, my husband, would it displease you to have our charming niece visit you this night to show you a mark of her affection? She has been talking of nothing else since her arrival here."

He scowled and nursed his bony chin. "But this she can do at a more seemly hour, Laurette. Tonight I am resolved to win that which I have labored for in vain since the day of our marriage."

"Yes, my lord husband," Laurette gave meek reply and fair cajoling smile, "and this is what prompts me to beg the favor of Marisia's presence here. For her grace and youth may stir you to performance of that great endeavor to which I look forward so impatiently myself."

"Well, well now," cackled the old fool, licking his lips in anticipatory relish, "in that case, I cannot begrudge the dear child this opportunity to signal unto me her happiness in the generous home I have provided. Indeed, I do think that her presence here will prove a happy augury for our future, for I find you marvelously humble and obedient, as I have not before."

"It is because I was affrighted by my undeservedly honorable estate as your good wife, my noble husband," was Laurette's adroit response, which naturally gratified the ego of the fatuous old idiot.

"Good, good, your humility has grace in my eyes. Then do you bring my niece to us straightaway," he purred.

No sooner said than done, and in a trice Laurette returned to the patron's bedchamber, leading the adorable raven-tressed Marisia by the hand. Eyes demurely downcast, clad only in her thin muslin shirt, which clung to her alluring young form in a manner that whetted the patron's narrowing, glittering eyes, she curtsied and murmured, "Dear uncle, I long to kiss you and my Tante Laurette goodnight ere I go to sleep."

"Sweet child, come to my arms, then," he cackled as he held them out. Marisia swiftly went to him and locking her slim ivory arms 'round his shoulders, tilted up her saucy face and bestowed an ardent and lingering kiss full upon his thin dry lips. But not content with this, she pressed her loins tightly against his and, arching on tiptoes, barefooted that she was like an innocent maiden led into a trysting chamber, slyly rubbed her fledgling mount against his sere, desiccated cock.

His face turned florid as he felt that lascivious constraint; till now, his hands had modestly rested on her shoulders. But when he felt the prodding of her bold, young, pear-shaped breasts against his chest and the wriggling friction of her loins, he grew emboldened enough to slip his hands down to the jouncy, high-set oval globes of her enchanting young backside, where one tentative squeeze of the satiny, firm flesh told him what a veritable houri of delights this untried maiden might well be.

"Mon dieu," he gasped in a voice even higher-pitched than usual due to his erotic excitement, "my sweet child, you recall to me the dear affection I had for your lamented mother, my adored sister Agnes. Ah, in her way, she was the loveliest maiden I had known, till, to be sure, the heavens smiled upon me by giving me your Tante Laurette!"

"Do you think I am pretty, dear Uncle Claude?" the bold young hoyden teased, not relinquishing hold with her arms, nor easing the subtle rubbings which she continued to inflict upon his tremoring loins with her own fledgling cunny and sweet belly.

"Aye, you are more than that, my sweet niece," he breathed, for his fingers were by now reveling in the palpation of her squirming bottom cheeks. "But it is high time you were abed, for your aunt and I must seek our nuptial privacy."

"Can I not stay to watch, dear Uncle Claude?" Marisia murmured, fixing him with her gray-green eyes in a look of exquisite enticement.

"Er—n-no, my child, it is not seemly," the patron stammered, giving Laurette an appealing glance to come to his aid in sending Marisia from their presence. But Laurette, the sly minx, only smiled and nodded graciously, saying, "See how she dotes on you, her dear uncle! She is a poor orphan now, and in need of affection!"

"That is true, but she is of too tender an age—" the old patron began, only to be interrupted by raven-haired Marisia, who, in a teasing voice, declared, "Oh, my uncle, I know well that you want to fuck Laurette, but I can help you do that if you will only let me stay!"

Monsieur Claude Villiers recoiled as if he were thunderstruck, his eyes virtually popping from their sockets. "Do I hear right?" he gasped. "How can it be that this fledgling speaks of the secret juncture between husband and wife in such lewd terms?"

"Because I know what fucking is, dear Uncle Claude," was the artful minx's reply, as she now put out a slim ivory hand and fondled the patron's cock through his nightshirt. "Do let me stay and watch, and I pledge I will help you both in your enjoyment!"

He stood there irresolute a moment, torn between his overweening lust and his residue of conscience and moralit.y. But Marisia tipped the scales in her favor by doffing her own nightshift and standing there adorably, bewitchingly, Lilith-nude. There was a soft, black down gathered over the dainty pink lips of her virgin cunny, yet, despite her youth, her body was voluptuous to the extreme. The boldly jutting young pears of her titties were crowned by soft, wide coral-tinted aureoles, and the paps which centered those delicious haloes were pert and saucy in their crinkly verve. The wide, shallow dimple of her belly seemed to wink salaciously at her bemused, astounded uncle. "Do you not think now I can aid you, my uncle?" Marisia pursued, her gray-green eyes sparkling with licentious merriment.

"Mon dieu, I do! Come then, my sweet niece and my beauteous young wife, and we shall seek a ménage à trois such as ne'er before mortal man delighted in," he swore.

Laurette slipped off her own nightshift, and now was milky skinned-naked as she clambered onto the bed on her proper side. Claude Villiers, shivering with feverish expectancy, hastened to expose his own scrawny nakedness and took his place beside her, whilst the ivory-limbed young niece nimbly stretched herself out at his right and, turning on her side, applied slim fingers to the dangling, dwindled edifice of his poor manhood.

"Oh, what enchantment, oh, what bliss," he babbled as he turned to the bosom of his wife, his bony fingers paddling at her superb, round milky bubbies, while gentle Laurette, forcing a beatific smile of humble acquiescence, let him do as he would.

"Oh, Uncle Claude, you must fuck Laurette soundly tonight, but your prick is not yet ready for that," Marisia murmured. "Yet, if I were a man, my dear aunt's beauty would make my prick stand to attention to dig into her darling cunt! Do let me help you fuck her, my uncle!"

"Do what you will," breathed the entranced old man, believing himself to have come somehow to Mohammed's paradise where, it is said, many lovely houris await the pleasure of the faithful. For, indeed, surrounded on both sides by two such delectable naked handmaidens, he felt himself capitulated into that glorious nirvana.

Marisia, giggling softly, rose to all fours, and, to his astonishment, placed herself in reverse over his lean, sere, naked body. Then, bending her head, she took up the dwarfed, dry head of her old uncle's cock between her soft red lips and sucked at it, while she lowered her fledgling cunny right over his florid, astounded face, so that his eyes might dote on the soft pink aperture scarcely shielded by the downy raven moss of her virgin pubis, as well as the sinuous amber furrow which parted the poutingly jutting cheeks of her ivory behind, and the dainty crinkly little rosette which lay at the end of that Sodomitic passageway.

"Marisia—ahh—ohh, what a darling child, to show her old uncle such delicious affection," the patron groaned. "I feel yet new life coming into my old bones—oh, continue the good work, and you shall have any boon you ask!"

"Yes, my sweet niece," Laurette counseled, "did I not tell you your dear Uncle Claude was generous to a fault? In gratifying him, Marisia dear, you do gratify me as well, for I am longing to have his good stiff cock visit my lonely well, and that as swiftly as possible!"

Now such converse, abetted by such lascivious yet charming, attonement, was ably planned to envigor the old patron, if, indeed, anything could at this late stage in his declining years. But Marisia, wishing to enthrall him totally, whispered, "Oh, my uncle, will you not pleasure me as well, since I am too young to feel the joy of a man's prick inside my little cunt, by kissing and putting your tonguc to it?"

Whereupon she took the head and some of the dwindled shaft into her mouth and rubbed the point of her pert little pink tongue all over the desiccated flesh.

Groaning with the sensations this naked young nymph was thus procuring for him, Monsieur Claude Villiers reached up his trembling hands and, gripping the pert bottom cheeks which undulated over his face, pulled Marisia's loins down to him. Then his quivering lips implanted on the fresh, sweet, pink tidbit of her virgin cunny a feverish kiss.

"Ooooooh, that feels so good, dear uncle," Marisia sighed languorously and lifted her head to regard Laurette and give her young aunt a conspiratorial wink. "But do not stop, and I will ready your rod to the delightful labor of fucking my beloved aunt!"

So saying, the artful little hoyden took hold of her uncle's organ with both hands and tickled and squeezed and stroked it, then directed the head once again between her lips, commencing an insistent suction. The old patron, shuddering and rolling his eyes, completely forgetting his lawful mate in this unexpected interlude, repaid Marisia in kind by kissing and sucking the soft pink petals of her fledgling quim, which soon began to palpitate and twitch and grow exquisitely swollen with the flux of blood to their erogenous volutes. Finding the tiny little love-button lodged in its protective nesting place of sweet, pink, soft cunny flesh, the patron jabbed it with the top of his tongue, causing Marisia to wriggle in the most salacious way and to accelerate and intensify the suction of her rosy soft mouth against his cockhead.

Now his organ had begun to stiffen to the largest state of erection I had observed since my entry into the Villiers household, and at last Marisia murmured, "It will soon be of a size sufficient to fuck my aunt's soft cunt, my dear uncle! Ohh, how nicely you are gamahuching me—oh, do rim me with your tongue!"

She had learned this lascivious lexicon from none other than her youthful swain, Everard, but at this point her elderly uncle had no thought of chiding her for such audacious bawdiness. Panting and gasping, he complied, and Marisia writhed and jerked her hips about as his tongue rasped into her maiden

crevice. Suddenly she uttered a squeal of ecstasy and
flooded his tongue with her girlish love-essence, proof
that she was hot-blooded beyond her tender years.

"Ohh, thank you, thank you, dearest, kindest
Uncle Claude," she breathed, as she rubbed her
tongue tip over his scrotum and balls, her bottom
cheeks still clenching yawningly in the aftermath of
amorous rapture, while long shivers rippled her slim
ivory thighs. "Ohh, now you are ready for my aunt, I
am sure of it! Quickly, let me help you put your big
strong prick into Tante Laurette's soft little cunt!"

She scrambled off the patron's shuddering body
leaving him in a magnificent state of turgidity, and
even Laurette's eyes widened at the unusual rigidity of
the staff sticking up between his lean thighs. But, at
Marisia's sign, she smiled and stretched herself in
sacrificial readiness upon her back, straddling her
thighs to their maximum, and holding up her arms to
her husband, while Marisia urged, "Come quickly,
Uncle Claude! Her cunt is hot and ready for your big
prick!"

Wheezing with his excitement, the scrawny old
man got on all fours and crouched over Laurette,
while the passionate Marisia took hold of the head of
his stiff cock with one hand and, gaping open the lips
of her young aunt's cunny with the other, introduced
husband to wife in the most exemplary way, as if she
had done it all her tender young life.

"Ohh, Laurette, Laurette, my darling pigeon, at
last, at last I shall fuck you!" he ecstatically announced
as he felt himself sink down into that tight, warm
channel. Her arms enfolded him and held him upon
her swelling, round milky bubbies, and her white
calves firmly clamped over his thighs to imprison him
to her love-bower.

Marisia did not take away her slim fingers till she
was certain that her aunt and uncle were truly fused.

Then, still excited, she knelt with her bottom resting on her heels, and slyly applied a forefinger to her moist, itching, pink cleft and began to frig herself as she watched the act of copulation.

Villiers' emaciated body was atremble with fulminating sensations; he arched himself, then sank back down, feeling his cock dig into the deeper recesses of his young wife's cunt. As for Laurette, though she still detested the old fool, her wakening the other night and her joyous plans to win Pierre Larrieu back to her side without her husband's knowledge had titillated her latent passions. More than that, the delicious salacity which her young niece had displayed had fanned the flames of her own carnal appetites and so the entranced old patron was able to call out in a hoarse, shaking voice, "Ohh, what paradise it is at last! Ohh, I can feel the walls of your soft cunt nibbling against my cock, my sweet pigeon, oh, my adored Laurette!"

But this gamut of sensations was too much for the boastful old fool; suddenly, his eyes rolled in their sockets, his head rose from her swelling teats, and he uttered a sobbing cry of "Oh, Ventre-de-Dieu. I have lost my spunk—ohh, I am undone, your tight cunt has robbed me of the long bliss I had dreamed of, wicked girl that you are!" And he sagged on her, giving down his seed.

When the patron had somewhat regained his consciousness and rolled off her, Marisia was there with dampened cloths to serve as sweet handmaiden to them both and to sponge them of the traceries of the brief fornication. It was then that the old fool, fixing Laurette with an inimical and suspicious glare, exclaimed, "Faithless hussy, you've tricked me and cuckholed me!"

"Nay, my dear husband, how can that be? You are the first man who has ever shot his seed into my womb," Laurette sought to mollify his wrath.

"Yet I have the proof, Laurette! A moment ago, when my cock engaged your cunt, there was no barrier to halt my advance! Your hymen is gone, but it was not perforated by my cock, and that you know full well!"

"My sweet husband, I am ashamed to tell you why that is so," Laurette murmured, lowering her beautiful blue eyes.

"I command that you tell me, you faithless, sluttish jade!"

"Do you not recall how I toiled in the wine cask that day of harvest, my husband?"

"Assuredly I do! That was the day I knew I must wed you—but, by my troth, you have stolen from me what is my right in bringing yourself as a virgin to my bed," he growled.

"But let me finish, my lord husband," petitioned Laurette, taking him by the shoulders and bestowing a gentle kiss of peace upon his lips. "You well know that I wished so much to win the prize that I trampled the good grapes with all my might and main. And it was the constant churning of my thighs that weakened the seal that was your rightful due and, alas, rent it asunder. It is only now that you have fucked me for the first time and made me truly yours that I dare pluck up my courage and overcome my natural shame to tell you of this woeful occurrence!"

And thus the imaginative golden-haired bride of the old patron showed that she could be as artful as Marisia, and, indeed, as the two zealous holy men who had taken such pains to "edify" her.

CHAPTER FOURTEEN

A week had passed since Marisia had entered into the Villier's household, and there was serenity in the heart of the patron of Languecuisse. When, on a Wednesday afternoon, Père Mourier and his confrère, Father Lawrence, came to visit the abode of Monsieur Claude Villiers to inquire after the spiritual welfare of both husband and wife, they were entranced to meet the raven-haired niece at the door in answer to their knock. For Victorine was gone on an errand on which Cupid smiled: Namely, to seek out Pierre Larrieu and inform him that young Madame Villiers proposed to meet him at midnight on that grassy knoll which had very nearly become the altar of their blessed reunion.

"But what a charming creature," exclaimed fat Père Mourier, glancing at his English colleague. "Tell me, my daughter, are you, as word has come to me, the ward now of the good Monsieur Villiers?"

"Oh, yes, Your Reverence. Have you come to see my uncle?

"To be sure, my child, and your aunt too. Are they at home?"

"My uncle is out in the fields supervising the planting of new cuttings for next year's harvest, Your Reverence. But my aunt is napping in her chamber," Marisia deferentially replied.

"What an intelligent and charming girl," Father Lawrence said. "Will you take us to her, my daughter?"

"Willingly, Your Reverence. Come this way."
Marisia led the way to Laurette's bedchamber, glancing
back to flash a saucy smile at both clergymen. And they
admired the supple play of her little young limbs and
backside against her thin frock.

Laurette, hearing voices, rose from her bed and
welcomed her obese Father confessor and his English
friend with shy blushes and curtsies, for she had not
forgotten the penance they had subjected her to. Yet,
contrary to what they might have feared, she bore
them not the slightest rancor.

"Ah, my dear child, you look radiant," Père
Mourier exclaimed.

"Thank you, mon père. But that is because my
dear husband and I have come to complete amity,"
responded Laurette.

"What glorious news, my daughter! Am I to
infer from that modest avowal that you have fulfilled
your obligations to the worthy patron?"

"Completely, Père Mourier."

"Oh, yes," innocently remarked the impertinent
raven-haired Marisia. "I myself saw them fucking and
my uncle declared himself quite overjoyed with Tante
Laurette's compliance."

"Tut, tut, tut, my child," gasped Père Mourier,
his florid face purpling at the sound of that vulgar
word, which summoned up the most erotic images in
his mind and flesh, "such things are not to be spoken
of so boldly. And you cannot have possibly witnessed
the holy act of union between man and wife."

"But she did, mon père," Laurette murmured,
"for it was at my husband's very invitation that she
attended our conjuncture."

"My child," Père Mourier gasped, staring avidly
at the impertinent minx, who tossed her head and
accorded him her most coquettish smile, "I cannot
believe you to be so mature!"

"And did you understand what was taking place?" asked Father Lawrence.

"Oh, yes, mon père," Marisia purred, making a charming moué with her soft red lips, "for I have watched the animals of the fields and barnyard making love, and, being so fond of my dear uncle, I wished to have him make my sweet Tante Laurette happy, too!"

"How precocious, how inspired," Père Mourier hoarsely declared. "Tell me, Madame Villiers, is it true that your husband means to adopt this enchanting creature?"

"So I have heard him say, mon père. And he will also bestow a gift of several thousand francs on your parish, that you may look upon my niece, Marisia, as one of your parishioners."

"The worthy Lord—did I not tell you, Father Lawrence, that here in Languecuisse we could boast of a noble benefactor whose thoughts are always for my poor flock?"

"That you did indeed, my most distinguished confrère," said the English ecclesiast, "and I shall never cease saying my benedictions for being guided to this humble rustic countryside to behold what miracles are wrought by devotion and faith and love!"

"But to her education," pursued the fat French priest. "Does he mean to see to this also?"

"As to that, mon père," Laurette swiftly invented, "I am sure he plans to beseech you to take Marisia under your wing and to give her education in the little school whose able mentor you are. Ah, she will be happy there, for I myself, as a child, did learn my alphabet and my geography in the same spot."

"My daughter, all my fears for your future have been banished," Père Mourier beamed, stealing covert glances at the lovely, raven-haired Marisia, who stood demurely by, her hands clasped and her eyes meekly downcast. "Perhaps the dear child would wish to accompany me to my rectory, to observe the very classroom in which she will acquire her wisdom under my humble direction."

"Of course, mon père," Marisia, after glancing at Laurette and winking, agreed.

"Then put on your cape, my child, for it may be chilly going through the fields," said the obese holy man. "Moreover, I wish to talk privately with your aunt."

Marisia left the room, and Père Mourier wrung his hands, a beatific smile on his fleshy lips. "Oh, my daughter, who would have thought such joy could have come to this household in so short a span of time? Now that you have set my mind at rest by avowing your fealty to the patron who places us all in his noble debt, I shall not again chide you over your past pinings for that rascal, Pierre Larrieu. Indeed, if you are discreet, my daughter, and bear M'sieu Villiers the heir he longs for, I shall not look to see if you chance upon this rogue—but take care I do not see it."

"Does Your Reverence, then, tolerate my meeting Pierre and chastely wishing him all happiness?" Laurette slyly queried.

Père Mourier shot a glance at Father Lawrence, then affably murmured, "Say that I shall do naught about it if I am not told of it, my daughter. I am indulgent too, you see. Yet this charming niece of yours, I feel, because of her precocity, needs guidance. If you will not balk at her being entrusted to my charge—oh, rest assured I shall not harm her—I will not balk either at your retaining some concern for your childhood friend."

Laurette came to him and took his hand and kissed it in token of meek submission to his will. Shortly thereafter the fat priest took his leave, Father Lawrence accompanying him, with Marisia between them, clinging to an arm of each of her ecclesiastical escorts.

I followed, amused at the flirtatious little plot which the two damsels had contrived, viewing whimsically the labyrinthine threat of Laurette's endeavors. She meant to have Pierre in her arms, I knew, and this without Monsieur Villiers' suspicion, now that he was enraptured over his young wife's complete and seemingly joyful surrender to such demands as his senile old cock could make upon her golden-furred cunt. And having found her niece to be of a furiously passionate nature, Laurette perceived that the lovely, raven-haired Marisia's trysts with Père Mourier would well provide the minx with ample opportunity to procure appeasement from the voracious carnal hungers that beset her fledgling loins, whilst at the same time, being the ward of the priest, Marisia would be able to afford idyllic moments for her own true swain, the youth Everard.

In the salon of the rectory, Père Mourier, after sending Desirée out to market, took Marisia on his knee and playfully interrogated her: "My child, you seem most alert and intelligent at first impression and I shall doubtless enroll you in my schoolroom in the highest possible form. But tell me now what you know of fucking, for this is a matter on which only the grownups, like your dear aunt and your illustrious uncle, are supposed to have knowledgeable opinions."

Oh, mon père, I've never been fucked myself," was Marisia's disarming, candid reply, "but a dear friend back in the village where I was born explained to me what prick and cunt were. Since I was too young to let him truly fuck me, mon père, I would frig him with my hands and my mouth. And he would do the same for my cunt, though once I let him rub just the head of his big prick over my spot."

"It is incredible how aptly gifted this dear child

is, do you not think so, Father Lawrence?" exclaimed the obese French clergyman.

"I am entirely of your opinion."

"Mon père, would you like me to show you what I did?" Marisia cooed.

"Yes, yes, by all means, my lovely child, so I may discover whether you did not unknowingly commit one of the unpardonable sins," he panted.

At this, the impertinent young baggage removed her frock and then her camisole. Then she finally let down her drawers, and stood ivory naked before the two breathless ecclesiastics. They could not speak, but the rigidity of their cocks spoke eloquently for them.

"Ohh, mon Dieu, what a big prick!" Marisia exclaimed as her eyes fixed on the projection from the front of Père Mourier's cassock. "May I gaze upon it and touch it, Your Reverence?"

"Willingly, my daughter," he gasped hoarsely as he removed his cassock and then his drawers. "Now then, show me precisely how it was that you and this bold youth played at fucking."

"It was like this to start, mon père," Marisia explained as she sank down on her knees and took hold of the fat priest's throbbing cock. Pressing a soft kiss on the heavy appendage, she wandered her slim fingers this way and that over his balls and scrotum.

"Ohhh, the sweet child! Ahh, what delicacy, what gentleness, Father Lawrence! She truly is incomparable, and yet, you see, she is naive and without sin. This is not truly fucking. Now, my daughter, let me see if I can grant you a little pleasure in return. Do you lie on the floor, exactly so." He crouched over the slim, ivory-skinned baggage, and, after stroking her belly and thighs, put his lips to her darling cunny. "Ahh, what sweet fragrance, like a flower of the woods," he rhapsodized. Then his pudgy forefinger began to tickle the lips of Marisia's cunny, while the agile young beauty, grasping his hairy, fat thighs, drew his huge rod down towards her mouth.

The pressure of her lips almost at once destroyed his self-control, for, with a hoarse shout of bliss, Père Mourier ejaculated huge gouts of viscous spunk, which Laurette's raven-haired niece managed, to the surprise of both incredulous men, to swallow without harm.

"Oh, I must try her," panted Father Lawrence, already naked and in most ferocious readiness as he clambered down over the naked young brunette in exactly the same way as his French confrère had done, and began to suck and tongue her dainty cunt. Marisia, giggling softly at the vagaries of two such superlatively adequate males, adapted herself to her new cavalier and began to suck on his massive cock head with such persistence that did not take him long to disgorge the molten lava in his vitals.

"Ahh, my enchanting child," Père Mourier murmured rapturously, "what absorbing studies we shall have. I shall coach you in all the sciences, and that of fucking also. Come, sit on my lap and tell me what you have learned of spelling and geography and history."

I remained a witness to an hour more of fondling, kissing and caressing. But it was not Père Mourier's intention, this first time, to subject the darling soft-lipped virgin cunny of Marisia to the brutal assault of his mighty cock. Yet I knew the time was not far off when he would breach her maiden defenses and exact the token of her ingenuousness.

That night, as the grandfather's clock in the hallway struck midnight, Laurette stole out of the patron's mansion to meet Pierre Larrieu. She and Marisia had lulled the old fool to sleep, the two of them robbing him of what little spunk he had managed to store up since that one act of fornication I have already related. And that was only accomplished by the dint of Laurette's fondling his cock whilst

218

Marisia licked it. In return, the patron generously
pledged Marisia that he would send to her village to
bring back Everard to work as a stable boy with
Hercule, his overseer.

***

It was a moonless night, and the darkness and
silence made an ideal trysting place of that grassy
knoll. And this time there was no scolding Père
Mourier to disturb the young lovers. With what joy did
Laurette remove her cape, standing only in filmy
nightshift which she permitted, blushingly, her young,
handsome, blond swain to remove, while she attached
his own garments with impatient fingers. Then, naked
the both of them, he holding her tightly against his
virile loins, kissing her face and lips with a thousand
ardent kisses, while her little hand fondled his massive
cock, they at last achieved the unison for which they
had longed. Sinking down on the grass, thighs spread
to welcome him, Laurette stared fondly up at his rigid,
angry-looking cock and breathed, "Oh, my darling,
tonight I shall truly become a woman for the first time.
My husband has had no real joy of me, for I have
saved myself for your dear cock, my beloved Pierre!"

He knelt down before her, his hands stroking her
thighs and belly and breasts. His forefinger at last
quested in the thatch of golden cunt curls, and began
to tickle the soft pink lips of her silt till she writhed
and gasped for him to attend her. But this Pierre
Larrieu was everything old Monsieur Claude Villiers
was not. Grasping her inner thighs with gentle
fingertips, Pierre tantalizingly rubbed the tip of his
rigid cock against the soft twitching lips of Laurette's
slit till she was almost frenzied with her lascivious
need of him. And only then, slowly, inch by slow inch,
did he sink his mighty blade between those greedily

clutching, soft pink labia, till at last their hairs merged and her arms clutched him savagely and her mouth glued to his as, masterfully, he began to arch and sink upon her in the inexorable, wonderfully exciting rhythm of a prolonged fuck.

Thrice they thus paid their tributes to Venus and Priapus while I watched over their happy beatitudes, ready to bite Pierre on the leg to warn him should some rude interloper like Père Mourier interrupt such passionate transports. But none did, and at last they parted with the sweetest of kisses and pledges to meet again, as I was sure they would.

Yet even I could not have predicted how soon that next meeting was to be, for, when Victorine timidly knocked at the old patron's bedchamber the next morning to ask if he wished his breakfast brought in on a tray, she found him lying there cold and lifeless, a beatific smile on his dry thin lips. The seizure of which Marisia had spoken had taken place; yet at last he had died a happy death, drawn to climax by young bride and younger niece, believing to the very end that his charming Laurette had overcome her aversion to him and come, finally, to love him for his own sake. And who is to say that illusion cannot sometimes be stronger than reality?

Two days later, after the funeral, Père Mourier attended the Widow Laurette Villiers, who was most becomingly attired in a simple black cotton dress, though she was now a wealthy and secure widow who need never again worry about a crust of bread or a roof over her head. For in his will the patron had left everything to her, save a thousand francs for Victorine.

"How can I console you in your terrible bereavement, Madame Villiers?" the fat French clergymen unctuously queried.

"Is it true that I am free to marry again? You have always told me it is better to marry than to burn."

"That is true, my daughter."

"Then I wish you to announce the banns between myself and Pierre Larrieu—after proper interval of mourning, to be sure."

"Oh, my daughter, this is madness!"

"Why so? Is he not the same flesh as my adored, lamented husband? Am I not lonely and in need of a strong young husband, that I may produce the heirs M'sieu Villiers so had his heart set upon?"

"Yes, but—"

"And, since I am heir to all this unexpected wealth, mon père, it is my wish to make free gift unto your parish of the little vineyard over which my dear father had tenancy. My parents will come to live with me in this big house. Oh, yes, and the rental on their cottage shall also be turned over for your charities, mon père."

"My daughter, I cannot bless you enough. Very well, you shall have you way. Perhaps it was thus intended." Père Mourier kissed Laurette, who then knelt to receive his blessing.

But, once outside, Father Lawrence caught him by the wrist. "A word with you, my confrère. I must go back to the seminary in England in a few days. Would it not be wise to entrust to me the care of that tender Marisia?"

"Why so?"

"Because the Widow Bernard, having grown used to a man about the house, longs to make confessional with you, Père Mourier. And you will have Desirée into the bargain. I go back a lonely man, without having contrived to save a single soul in all my time in France."

Père Mourier frowned, considering: "There is merit in what you say, mon confrère. But I should grieve over the loss of that delicious, forward minx."

"True, and I know with what vigilance you seek

to guard the souls of the young. Yet take heart. In our seminary, we have many lovely young novices, even more adept and ardent than the charming Marisia. I have long felt that I should induce the Father Superior to send some of these well-edified daughters to another country, where they may expand their education. And I will see to it that several of them are sent to the parish school of Languecuisse."

"On that case, take her and with my blessing. Ah," Père Mourier exhaled a nostalgic sigh, "how I shall miss the minx! Those soft lips, that nimble tongue, that eagerness to learn which characterizes her."

"She will return to you even better edified, I promise," smilingly retorted the English ecclesiastic.

And thus it was decided. On the very next evening, Laurette said a tender au revoir to her raven-haired young niece, who, when Father Lawrence had presented himself to ask to take her back to the seminary of St. Thaddeus as novice, had herself enthusiastically pleaded with her aunt to let this happen. And Laurette, perhaps wisely realizing that the presence of the precocious girl in the household where now strapping, handsome young Pierre Larrieu would be lord and master might be highly precarious to her own hopes for marital fidelity with her adored spouse, gave her leave.

Now that I knew the end of the story, I was drowsy. I had chosen my napping place in the golden tendrils of Laurette's sweet cunt curls. And that was why I was not aware of Laurette's telling her niece that she wished to give her a parting remembrance of their joys together. Taking a pair of dainty scissors, Laurette cut off some of those golden ringlets and encased them in a little locket with a golden chain, which she hung about the ivory neck of her niece.

And so, when I woke, I found myself—to my

great horror—imprisoned in that locket!

And then I heard the resonant, mellow voice of Father Lawrence close by, telling Marisia that they would arrive in London a few days hence, where she would be initiated as a novice, he being her sponsor. That was why she had forsaken her memories of Everard. Competent though that distant youth might be—and, as you well know, I never had the chance to conjecture—Marisia had already decided that the mighty cock of her newfound protector could not easily be surpassed. And as she whisperingly confided to him, replying to his statement, "Oh, Your Reverence, I ask only one boon, that before I am made novice, you, all by yourself, will initiate me with your great, wonderful prick, and show me truly what fucking really is!"

What irony! I, the imaginative, sophisticated Flea who had vowed never to see Bella and Julia and those licentious men of the cloth, was now on my way back to their very lair, entrapped in the curls of the young virgin I had befriended. Was that to be my reward?

I told myself philosophically that all was not forever hopeless. A Flea can live a long time without nourishment. I was sure that tender Marisia would at some time or another open her locket to recall those happy hours with her golden-haired young aunt. Then I might escape and try my fortunes in some other still more distant land.

Yet, what if she does not open the locket? What if, just as at this very moment when I hear the soft sloshing of tongue within mouth, and mouth greedily accepting tongue, and the hoarse whispers and the soft giggles of that novice-to-be and her expert sponsor, Marisia, in her greedy desire to learn what fucking truly is, forgets Laurette?

What then?